MW00977833

8/19

Longitude: Zero Degrees

Zero Degrees

The second in the Quimbaya Trilogy

Dianne C. Stewart

bean pole books

2009

Beanpole Books
P.O. Box 242
Midway, Florida 32343

Printed in the United States of America on acid-free paper
First Edition

Editor: Katherine Forrest
Cover designer: Kiaro Creative

ISBN-10: 0-9667359-4-3
ISBN-13: 978-0-9667359-4-9

As always, for my family: Tim, Steve and Nicky

Acknowledgments

I am grateful again to Beanpole Books for support and the creative freedom to write exactly the story I wanted to tell.

Many thanks to Katherine V. Forrest, whose expert editing helped Liv, Cal, and Anthony be at their best; special thanks to Julia Watts for suggestions and encouragement; finally, a most particular thanks to the pets who have owned me over the years and inspired the animal characters in this book.

Prologue

Fall of 1763, twenty miles east of Barbados

Maskelyne's nerves were frayed to threadbare, and he had come up on deck to be alone.

The two-masted British schooner glided through sparkling aquamarine waters in the far western Atlantic, leaving a graceful wake as she picked up speed to eight knots. At less than one hundred tons, she could run even faster on days when the wind was favorable and her square topsail was removed from the bowsprit and hoisted up the foremast.

Maskelyne rested his elbows on the deck rail and frowned at the sight below: a kelp forest, anchored in the sandy bottom and waving underwater like a woman's hair in a liquid breeze. Above the surface, an azure sky punctuated by puffy cumulus clouds met shades of turquoise sea, from palest cyan to deep teal.

None of it held appeal for him—not even the ship, elegantly rigged with twin sails, suspended from spars reaching all the way from the tops of the masts toward the stern. Other passengers carried on about the sails' beauty, but he refused to join in their drivel. There was nothing pleasurable about this voyage.

Sir Nevil Maskelyne, *Astronomer Royal* by appointment of His Majesty George the Third, had completed his mission with stunning success, though any *Huzzah!* greeting him on his return home would be shouted in honor of his enemy.

By order of the king, Maskelyne's island observatory had tested the accuracy of the new timepiece, the latest creation of his rival, John Harrison. If the watch, nicknamed "H4," kept good time, Harrison's career and accomplishments might outshine his own.

And the awful gadget had performed three times better than required.

Now the past two months of Maskelyne's life would benefit the man he hated. He should have spent this time in England, finishing his *Almanac* and convincing the Board to forget Harrison and use his own lunar-distance method to find longitude. Soon, Harrison would be heaped with praise for finding a brilliantly simple way to determine longitude: the use of an accurate timepiece.

The astronomer was in a mood to despise everything—especially John Harrison, though the macaw digging her claws into his shoulder might also gain that distinction if she bit him again. Deceptively named Precious, she was getting a free ride to England at the express command of His Majesty, who had requested a parrot as a gift for the Queen.

He leaned out over the water. Maybe the nuisance would fall off or blow away. Precious responded with a nip to his ear and a further tightening of claws. He winced, and his spirits plunged to a new low.

He'd endured food poisoning from an outdoor fruit market and bloody fingers from the pecking of this miserable bird. After steaming like a plum pudding in the August heat, he felt limp and soggy from the torrents of rain that had battered the island as the season of tropical storms began working toward its autumn peak.

His insufferable assistant had refused to act properly subordinate and was no longer speaking to him, which made the atmosphere in their tiny cabin unpleasant. He was tired of hot sunshine, tired of the rain, tired of everybody being foreign. Why couldn't they all just be English?

And the insects. He shuddered as he thought about what had probably crawled on his skin nightly as he'd endured life in a strange land among people and plants he'd never seen before, eating food he wasn't used to and watching his entire future slip away.

The single agreeable thing left was the cleanliness of the crew and ship. He himself was a fastidious person, and he'd noted with relief that the sailors appeared healthy, with no evidence of scurvy. The galley crew scrubbed and scoured the cooking pots, and the bowls and spoons were wiped clean with a cloth, dipped in a bucket of seawater that was changed every day.

It pleased him, too, that the sailors had carefully careened the ship while they were moored in Barbados, scraping seaweed and barnacles from the hull until it was perfectly smooth. He'd complimented the captain on how fine it looked, then nearly had a fainting spell when he heard why a clean hull was important: to help the ship outrun pirates.

"A schooner's a wise choice when moving through pirate territory," the captain had said, crinkling his weathered face into a smile and pulling at his bushy beard with a calloused hand. "She has a shallow draft and she's easy to maneuver."

He continued, as Maskelyne fervently wished he hadn't begun the conversation: "We have a slight advantage of speed, since we're not loaded down with cannons as they are."

Maskelyne was uncertain how a little extra speed compensated for a lack of arms and hoped they wouldn't have to test the captain's theory.

He sighed and stared at the horizon from the side of the boat. He never wanted to look back at Barbados again, and the prospect of going home to battle Harrison was daunting. The clockmaker's innovation would likely change the world and might cost Maskelyne his rightful place in history. Bitterness welled up in him like a fire, sending fingers of flame from his stomach to his throat.

He thought of the H4 watch, now in a small wooden crate safely packed in the trunk beside his bunkbed. One thing seemed certain— never again would a bit of metal in a box alter the course of history as this one would.

Chapter One

"I can't, Coach—there's nothing I can do about it."

Liv Wescott carefully pushed the "Off" button, then slammed the phone onto the stand. There, that felt better.

She banged her fist on the countertop. Why was this her fault? She was the natural choice for girls' soccer captain at Jefferson Bainbridge Middle School, so she'd said yes to Coach Donnelly's offer, knowing that summer practices were part of the package and choosing to believe she'd be there for them.

Should she have known her father would accept the assignment to London? What if her family had stayed right here in Adelaide Village and she'd let someone else have the job she deserved? To be fair, Dad had hinted that they might make the ten-week move, but Liv had seen no reason to shape her summer plans on a maybe.

So she'd made some commitments, and now it was all falling apart. This phone call was her fourth confrontation in as many days.

She'd apologized to the school chorus director who complained because Liv was accompanist and wouldn't be in town for a couple of important summer rehearsals.

She'd felt genuine guilt when her piano teacher had blinked and said, "You'll miss a lot of lessons."

When she'd broken the news to Mr. Harper, English teacher and debate team coach, she'd bitten her lip to stifle her anger at his response. "If you had let me know before school was out, Olivia, I could have had tryouts for your spot on the team. But now the seventh-graders have scattered for the summer, and we were planning on regular practices, as you already knew. . ."

She knew! She knew! Hot tears raced down her cheeks as she turned back to the avocado and pickle sandwich she'd been making before the phone rang. What was wrong with everyone, anyway? She stuffed potato chips into a plastic storage bag and beat them with her fist into tiny crumbs, pouring them straight out of the bag and onto the avocado slices while considering her options.

She could go out and work on soccer moves, but of course she hated soccer at this moment. She could pound out a few frustrations on the piano except, come to think of it, she hated the piano right now, too.

Run. That's what she'd do. Run until her lungs screamed so she wouldn't have to scream. Run until she thought of something to say to the people who had the nerve to think she'd let them down.

The click-clack of toenails on the tile floor alerted Liv to a doggy presence. Southpaw trotted into the kitchen, head up, ears alert.

"Hey, boy." Liv reached down and patted the golden retriever's smooth chest. "Do you want to go for a run?"

Southpaw answered her question with one of his own, locking his eyes on Liv's sandwich and moaning. She pulled a piece of avocado from the seven-grain bread slices. He vacuumed it from her fingers, chewed once, and let the drool-drenched blob fall to the floor.

Liv had to smile as she picked up the mess. "Sorry, I know you're a carnivore. Forgive me?" Southpaw wagged his tail, then loped away to answer a knock at the kitchen door.

On the back porch, smiling and waving, was Cal Bradley. I'm in no mood to put on a good front for him, thought Liv, walking to unlock the door and taking several hits from Southpaw's thrashing tail. I need time to be angry—about having to go, about teachers who think I need to make their backup plans. And I don't want to hear him rattle on about how awesome this trip is going to be. A scowl darkened her face as her twin brother's best friend burst into the kitchen.

"Anthony just called! You're going to London—London, England! And I'm invited!" He dropped to the floor and wrestled Southpaw, who was excited to see someone excited. They rolled and tossed until Southpaw covered Cal's face with slobbery kisses.

"That's it! You win. How about a belly rub?" Southpaw melted onto the floor and stuck his left front paw in the air as Cal rubbed him. Cal looked up at Liv and saw her brimming tears. The scowl had turned into a tight-lipped frown.

"Whoa, what's up, Liv? I've never seen you like this."

It was true, she thought ruefully. Liv Wescott, rising seventh-grader at Jefferson Bainbridge Middle School, or Bridge Mid, with emphasis on rising. Fearless, bossy, a leader—never weak enough to cry in front of anyone else.

"They think they can just pack us up along with their suitcases and plop us down on the other side of the Atlantic for three months! I have obligations! I have soccer, debate team, chorus accompanying—at least I used to. Everybody's mad at me right now, and it's not fair!" She stopped, embarrassed by her outburst, but enjoying a chance to be unreasonable.

Cal stopped rubbing Southpaw and stood up. "Look on the bright side, Liv. This is a great trip! I have obligations, too, so I'm planning ahead. Jacob Stockton may get to be basketball captain now that I can't practice this summer, but Anthony says we can take his laptop and I've found some online basketball playbooks and drills. I'll run in the parks to stay in shape—you can, too!"

"It's not that easy," sniffed Liv. "You have basketball to think about. I'm being pulled in four different directions. I don't mean it as a put-down, Cal. I just have more to deal with than you do. I don't expect you to understand." She stared at her sandwich, her appetite gone.

Cal's smile was knowing. "Oh, I understand. You're used to being in charge and being a winner. You're tough on yourself and on everyone else."

That drew her full attention. He continued, "So, you have a lot going on? It's all manageable. People play soccer in London. There has to be someplace you can practice. And pianos! They have pianos in London, too. Have you asked your parents to help you find a place to practice while you're there, or were you too busy being mad?"

He paused, pulling handfuls of golden dog hair from his navy Bridge Mid Beagles shirt and shorts. Southpaw, inexhaustible source of spare fur, stayed immobilized on the floor with his eyes closed. Cal stroked him with the toe of a running shoe.

Liv picked up her sandwich and nibbled at the crust. "Go on, I'm listening."

"Debate team is trickier, but you can get some topics from Mr. Harper and email your arguments to the team. And why couldn't they email you back? It'll keep your skills sharp and show Mr. Harper you're trying."

Liv took a bite, chewed slowly, then said, "How'd you get to be so smart?"

Cal's only answer was a grin. He rose to his feet. "Now, Anthony and I are going to start planning our London adventure. A nice, normal adventure..." His voice lowered to a whisper, . . . "with no time travel."

Liv watched him disappear up the stairs. He was right. She could face anything—she had time traveled. She, Anthony and Cal had journeyed to the past. They'd changed history, and no one else knew. Well, almost no one.

That put her problems into perspective. Temporary inconveniences. She said to Southpaw, "Let's go, boy!" He responded by running to the wall peg where his retractable leash hung.

Chapter Two

A two-mile run was just right for Liv. She was sweaty and feeling great. She'd gone full-out most of the way, slowing down only when Southpaw stopped to sniff bushes and trees.

Back at the house, Mrs. Wescott finished scrubbing peeled baby carrots for Liv's eighteen-month-old sister, placed them in a bowl on the table, then heaved Anna's booster seat onto a chair and whisked Anna into it in one deft motion.

Liv admired her mother's efficient movements. She was just as graceful and in control as she had been while she was a children's clothing executive, before Anna's birth. Liv noted that Anna's bib looked new. Probably Mom's latest design. She had a feeling it wouldn't be long till her mother was back in the business. Liv smiled and hummed a tune as she headed upstairs.

Fresh from a shower and dressed in her favorite jeans shorts and Gap T-shirt, Liv opened the hall closet door and shoved her wet running clothes and towel down the laundry chute. Laughter came through the open door of Anthony's room and she followed the sound.

Anthony sat cross-legged on the floor, typing into his laptop, while Cal sprawled on the bed looking over his friend's shoulder at the screen. Anthony raised his head to glance at Liv. "If you're looking for Southpaw, he's hiding out from Anna."

She followed the direction of his nod and saw a golden tail sticking out from under the bed. Anthony closed his laptop and reached up to the nightstand for a bag of chips. She accepted them, rattling the bag to be sure Southpaw heard. When nothing happened, she opened the bag and pulled one out, waving it around to spread the aroma.

"Chips are his favorite," said Liv. "Maybe he's stuck."

Cal leaned over the opposite side of the bed until his head touched the floor and lifted the bottom of the bedspread for an upside-down view of Southpaw, then slid off the bed and rejoined Anthony and Liv.

"He's in there pretty tight and his eyes are popping out. I hope he can breathe." Cal lifted the foot of the bed at one corner, and Liv jumped to her feet to help him with the other.

Anthony called out, "Be careful! I just put the box in there yester—"

A sharp clunk was followed by the sound of dog elbows and hind toenails on the wooden floor under the bed. Southpaw was moving, but not toward them. Anthony grasped the disappearing tail with one hand and reached for a leg with the other one.

Liv asked, "While you're pulling him out, want to explain why you moved the box from our agreed hiding place?"

Anthony grimaced and inched the dog a little closer. "He found it under the guest room bed and brought it to me. I hid it in my closet with some shoes, then behind my bookcase, and he found it there, too. He's gotten the scent of it now and he thinks it's a game!"

Anthony ignored Liv's stare and said, "Well, he's a retriever, right? Anyway, I stuck it up here between a couple of slats, and everything was okay until now. Wait a minute—I have him around his middle. Come on, boy."

Southpaw emerged, covered with dust, with the box in his mouth. Liv and Cal gasped together, and Anthony remained perfectly still.

Liv recovered first. "Here boy, bring it to me. Come on."

With a wag of his tail that sent dust bunnies flying like dandelion fluff in the wind, Southpaw came, holding his treasure. "There you go, just let me have it. That's right. Oh, no! Anthony, you didn't tape it shu—"

The catch on the front of the box was undone. They watched as two little doors swung apart, revealing a set of drawers. The box didn't work for everyone, but for some it allowed the holder to time travel, the year determined by the combination of opened and closed drawers. Southpaw lowered his head, and gravity pulled two of the drawers open. Liv lunged for him, held on with all her strength, and closed her eyes.

She'd expected to skin her elbows on the scratchy pile of Anthony's indoor putting mat. Instead, she opened her eyes to find herself and Southpaw inches deep in spongy leaf mold, the odors so pungent she could taste them. Filtered sunlight dribbled through a canopy of green. They were in a forest. Southpaw barked, too thrilled with all the new smells to be bewildered by the change of scenery.

Keeping him in a full dog-hug, Liv looked around for the box. There it was. Southpaw had released it from his jaws. The drawers marked thousands and hundreds and were opened to the notches for one and six, so they were somewhere around the year 1600.

It was just out of her reach. Southpaw squirmed to get free, and two beady eyes stared at them, their owner slowly raising its black-and-white-striped tail. Liv's brain processed all that information in a millisecond, including the distance to the skunk— about five feet.

But she hesitated. She needed to secure the dog, reach for the box, and somehow manage to get the drawers closed. That would take them back to the present. Would her movements upset the skunk?

Southpaw saved her from having to find out by giving a loud "Woof!" followed by a low growl in his throat. Liv reacted fast this time, sliding the fingers of her left hand around his collar and reaching for the box with her right.

Only when she held the box safely in her grasp did she look in the direction Southpaw now faced, to the right of the skunk. Standing in partial shadow, not ten feet away, was a full-grown man with copper-colored skin. Bare-chested, he wore a deerskin loincloth and carried a small bow with two arrows. His obsidian-black hair was pulled back from his face into a ponytail and held by a rawhide strip.

He was clearly astonished by their presence—his mouth gaped open and his forehead wrinkled into a frown. Afraid to break eye contact, Liv returned the Brave's stare. Would a smile or wave be a sign of weakness? Could he reach them before she closed the box?

Southpaw strained against Liv's hold on his collar, ready to attack. His movement broke the standoff. Liv ducked to adjust her grip, and an arrow whizzed past her ear.

She saw his hand tremble as it gripped the second arrow. He was as nervous as she was! Even so, she couldn't be lucky enough for him to miss twice. Liv forced herself to swallow her fear and push the drawers closed.

Through the blur, she watched the skunk, displeased at losing his first target, shift his aim toward the Brave and register his opinion.

Chapter Three

"If I were speaking to you, which I'm not, I'd start by saying that any moron would have taped the drawers shut after the first time the golden retriever outsmarted him!"

Liv was back in Anthony's bedroom, on a tirade. Southpaw had fled downstairs, and a terrarium-like smell lingered in the room.

"Next, I'd say that if the retriever did it three times, your average moron would have gotten the box out of the house and let his friend take it." She offered the box to Cal, who accepted it without protest, avoiding eye contact.

Anthony turned back to his laptop. "Yeah, well, at least I have a friend."

It was true. She could count her acquaintances by the dozen, but it wasn't easy to operate near the force of nature that was Liv without getting tossed around a little. It wasn't like laid-back Anthony to shoot off a retort, and the silence between them grew, while Cal shifted in his seat.

Finally, Liv spoke. "That's cold."

Anthony rubbed his hand over his face. "I know. I'm sorry,

Sis. I'm sorry I put you in real danger. I'm glad you're okay." He walked over to her and gave her a hug, then brushed forest debris from her shoulders. "Brush off your own backside—it's covered with dirt, too."

Anthony's trademark grin reappeared. "Since you seem to be speaking to me again, you can fill us in on how you came by that dirt, and if we need to do anything about it."

"If you mean did I change history—no, I don't think so." Liv chuckled in spite of herself. "Unless you count one very surprised skunk and the really unhappy Brave who got sprayed instead of Southpaw and me. We may have accidentally added to the Native American folklore, but other than that, no harm done."

The three of them let out a collective sigh of relief. It could have been much worse. When Cal had discovered the box containing the ancient South American gold medallion in an old house last year, they had begun what seemed at first like harmless adventures.

But the golden disk from the mysterious Colombian treasure of the Quimbaya had tempted them. It hadn't taken long to graduate from sightseeing in the past to trying to prevent disasters, and they soon learned that even the best actions can bring unintended consequences. There was no way to sleuth out every detail of how the world was changed now because of them. They weren't even sure they wanted to know.

The silence was comfortable now. They'd long since talked things out and said everything there was to say on the subject.

It was Liv who broke it. "Okay, guys, time to get organized. We can start with some group ideas—where to go, what to do. Hold on—I'll get my iPhone." She moved toward the door, stopping to pull a twig from her hair and drop it into Anthony's trashcan.

Anthony squirmed. "No offense, but Cal and I were making our own plans." He raised the cover of his laptop. "Check this out: Sir John Soane's Museum. Old Sir John was an architect who collected cool stuff. It says on Wikipedia that he bought the sarcophagus of Seti I for his house!" He clicked on a diagram of the museum. "We ran across it while we were surfing the Web for places to go. An Egyptian tomb in your basement—wow." He sighed.

Liv left them to it. She might as well throw her running clothes into the washer. She could come back in a few minutes, and no doubt Anthony would have led Cal through several more Web sites, maybe even coming up with a few that would interest her. As she headed down the hall, she heard him exclaim, "Look at that ship. It's loaded!"

After a quick spin of the dial to Warm-Cold/Permanent Press, Liv bounded up the basement steps, two at a time. She ascended the main stairs and approached her brother's room. Their backs were turned to her, and Liv heard Cal ask, "Not even a closet or a drawer?"

Anthony replied, "No, Southpaw would just sniff it out and scratch and whine. That would give the housesitter a reason to snoop." Liv hesitated at the threshold.

Cal continued, "Not my house. My mom says they're going to pull everything out of my room to paint while I'm gone. She's even talking about painting my furniture, so there's not one safe place to hide anything in my room. I'm so tame and lame I usually have nothing to hide, and I'd like to keep it that way."

Liv stepped into the room and reclaimed her seat on the beanbag. Anthony looked from his friend to his sister, then to the old wooden box. "That settles it, then. We take it with us."

Cal asked, "Um, isn't that maybe a little impulsive? I'm thinking there are several ways for things to go wrong if we leave the box here, but more like thousands of ways if we take it with us."

Anthony shook his head. "If something happened here, what could we do about it? It's worth the risk to keep the box with us—keep it from getting into the wrong hands. If either of you has a better plan, now's the time to share. I'm all ears." He closed his laptop and turned to face them.

Cal sighed. "I can't believe I'm agreeing to this, but it beats worrying every minute if our hiding place was good enough. What do you think, Liv?"

Liv reached out and ran her finger over the top of the box, tracing the mother-of-pearl inlay in the dark wood. "I think our trip just got a lot more complicated."

Chapter Four

The Wescott family van cruised along the interstate, headed for the tri-county airport. They had picked up Cal at his house only five minutes before, and already Liv was wishing she could toss him out at the next red light.

"I just think maybe it shouldn't be in my suitcase—that's all I'm saying," he whispered, his fake smile looking worse than none at all. "What if it doesn't go right through security? This stuff drives me crazy, and I don't ad-lib well under pressure."

Anthony grinned and clapped Cal on the shoulder as if his friend had said something witty. Sitting in the rear seats of the van, they could talk without being overheard by the grownups in front, but they could be seen, and Cal looked on the verge of losing it.

Liv sat in the middle row with Anna. She grabbed the baby's sandal and began playing with the toes in it. "This little piggy went to market—it's going to be okay, Cal."

"Yeah? Should I say it's a gift if they ask me about it?"

"This little piggy stayed home—they won't ask you, Cal."

"Are you sure the rubber band around it will hold? Maybe

we should have taped the whole thing shut."

"This little piggy had roast beef, and this little piggy had none—the rubber band looks like we have nothing to hide. Taping just the drawers shut was enough."

"What if our luggage gets lost? Then what?"

"And this little piggy cried, 'Wee, wee, wee, all the way home!'" She replaced the first foot. Anna stuck out the second one. "That's what we'll do, I guess. Cry. Now, look happy—my parents are watching in the rearview mirror!"

Ten weeks to get through without choking Cal. It was going to be a long summer.

The artificial winter in Hartsfield-Jackson International Airport blasted from vents above their heads, belying the June Atlanta heat. Liv, Anthony and Cal had been instructed to walk up the jetway and wait for Mr. and Mrs. Wescott while they reclaimed Anna's stroller from gateside baggage check.

The connecting flight from Adelaide Village had been uneventful. The box had breezed through security, swaddled in Cal's socks and underwear, right in the center of his suitcase. So far, so good.

Even Anna had posed no problems. Just a bit fussy from air pressure changes while the plane gained altitude, she'd taken a drink from her sippy cup, smiled, and gone right to sleep on her dad's shoulder. With Anna refreshed, the rest of the journey was sure to be interesting.

Now that Liv was used to the idea of going, she found herself looking forward to the trip. Mr. Harper had been surprised but agreeable when Liv suggested debates by email, and had complimented her on a creative solution to the team's scheduling problems.

Her father had made arrangements for her to practice piano at the home of Mr. Havard, a barrister he would be working with in London. "Two grand pianos in their living room—can you imagine?" her mother had said.

Soccer was going to have to take care of itself, but Liv could jog in Kensington and Hyde Parks to stay in shape while Mrs.

Wescott walked with Anna in the stroller. And Mr. Havard had another suggestion.

"He says," her dad had related with a twinkle in his eye, "that if you're any good, there are always people playing soccer in the parks, and someone would probably let you join in their game. I told him you weren't good, you were outstanding."

It was true, and she had the trophies and ribbons to prove it. But knowing her dad, he would have been just as proud of her if she were a complete klutz, as long as she tried. She never felt pressured to excel to please her parents. No, she was driven because she was Liv.

But right now she could enjoy herself. Things were under control, just the way she liked them, and the pace of the huge airport made her pulse quicken.

The group reunited and proceeded along the wide corridor, following the signs to the international concourse. Mrs. Wescott led the way with the empty stroller, and Mr. Wescott followed close behind with Anna on his shoulders. Liv, Anthony and Cal walked single file, three abreast—whatever the human traffic tide allowed.

Liv was absorbed by the passing parade moving in all directions, dressed for destinations of work or play. Business types spoke in serious tones on cell phones, passing and dodging as they talked. An elderly couple chatted with the driver of their motorized cart, while a little girl in braids with motion-activated light-up shoes hopped from terrazzo square to square with both feet.

And the stores—dozens of them. Most made sense to Liv: luggage, books to read on the plane, DVD rentals, souvenirs. But perfume? Who would open a whole store just for perfume in an airport? If she were running a store here, she'd sell stuff that everybody needed, or at least wanted.

Down the escalator they went, passing by the waiting train and choosing instead to tunnel their way through the underground region on the moving sidewalk. They stood single file on the huge conveyor belt.

Anthony looked up and down the expanse of rubber. "This

must be what it's like for a jar on an assembly line." He circled his arms in front of himself. "You travel down the belt, a big funnel opens up, and before you know it you're full of mayonnaise, or cocktail onions or pickled anchovies." He staggered under the imaginary weight. "A pair of giant tongs comes down and twists a lid on you." He jerked his head sideways. "A hand reaches out and sticks a label on you." He slapped his stomach. "Then they pack you in a box."

He hopped off the break in the moving sidewalk and made his way toward the middle area where the floor was just a floor. Liv and Cal followed, and the three of them powerwalked. They chugged their arms like locomotive engines, then slowed down to let Anna and her parents beat them, cheering for her while her dad held her aloft.

Emerging from the up escalator, the group made their way toward their assigned gate, stopping only once when they realized they'd lost Anthony. Liv spun around.

"There he is, in front of the glass exhibit. I'll go back for him and meet you at the gate." She sprinted back.

"Didn't know you were a Chihuly fan." Liv put her arm through Anthony's, admiring the luminous pieces in the display case. Anthony was rooted to the floor. His eyes fluttered closed, and he inhaled and exhaled a long, luxurious breath.

"I think I'm in love—Shh. . ."

He pointed upward, where a syrupy female voice flowed from unseen speakers, admonishing travelers to ". . .please ruh-fra-ain from smoking."

"She's probably forty years old and a chain-smoker, Anthony. Let's go."

"Ugh, thanks for the image. Give me a second to poke out my mental eye." He stuck his finger in the center of his forehead and let his sister lead him toward the gate.

Liv smiled at her brother, the only romantic in a family of overachievers. "Hey, she breaks your heart, you let me know. I'll beat her up."

They arrived at the seating area of their departure gate to

find almost no one sitting down. A young woman, her mass of auburn curls lacquered into perfect submission and her navy uniform stiffly starched, leaned toward a microphone and spoke in cordial tones: "Now that our first-class passengers, as well as platinum, gold, and silver, persons needing assistance, and those traveling with small children have boarded, we invite passengers seated in zone three to come forward."

Liv wondered how anyone could be left in the airport after all that, but a substantial crowd remained, and the "pardon me"s began. The cluster split like an asymmetrical amoeba. Zone Three surged forward, narrowed and elongated into a single-file line. The larger part of the amoeba remained behind, swirling and churning as passengers checked their tickets and determined where they should be in the mass.

As the starched young woman called more and more zones until the gate area was almost deserted, the elder Wescotts hung back. They answered the call for Zone Nine with quiet nonchalance. "They've shifted to Get Anna Settled mode," Liv explained in hushed tones to Cal as she picked up her backpack and tucked it under her arm. "If we start helping her wind down now, she may sleep her way across most of the ocean. Don't talk to her much or play with her, okay? And don't act excited."

"I can't help it—I am excited. I've never been so far away from home, to someplace so different." Cal's voice was low-volume but animated. Liv laughed and shook her head.

"Am I still not calm enough?" he asked.

"It's not that, Cal. I was just thinking—you've been captured by a pirate, saved lives, traveled to worlds that aren't supposed to exist. I'd call that far away and different. It's cool you can be thrilled about a trip that just crosses an ocean. Good for you. Now, walk behind Anthony, copy him, and you'll be fine."

The plane was nearly full when they boarded. The auburn-haired lady had glided from microphone to ticket scanner in the terminal and now stood in the cabin, directing traffic as passengers stepped inside. "First class to the left, please, coach to the right."

"Riff-raff to the right—that's us, team," Mr. Wescott joked. It was fine with Liv. Who wanted to march past plush leather seats and yards of legroom before folding yourself up into a pretzel? They moved forward, claimed their seats and settled in.

Chapter Five

It was time for Liv to give up the window seat. She'd begun the flight at the aisle, with Anthony in the middle and Cal by the window. The plan was to shift every hour until lights out, sleep where they landed, then renegotiate at wake-up time.

So back to the aisle for now, the perfect time for a restroom break. She left Anthony and Cal resettling and advanced to the set of water closets at the front of the coach section. Both occupied. Liv stood, wondering if she'd be in the way when the doors opened.

The three bulkhead seats at the right window were all empty, so she lifted the armrests out of the way and stretched across, feet up and pointing toward the aisle. Somber navy drapes prevented peeking into first class.

Remembering that Cal's mom had advised the three young people to stand up every thirty minutes during the flight so they wouldn't get deep vein thrombosis, she felt a wave of sympathy for Cal. No wonder the kid could be neurotic sometimes. But... what if his mom was right? Liv lifted her feet and flexed her ankles, one at a time, then grasped an ankle and held it at shoulder height with bent knee. By the time she had done both legs, she had an audience.

The person looking at her had passed through the first class curtains and was about to enter the restroom, just in front of her. Their eyes met and Liv looked away, embarrassed to be caught doing something so goofy. She leaned forward and pulled a travel magazine from the holder on the side of the bulkhead, pretending to be interested in the table of contents and conscious of the fact that the man had seemed even more eager than she to turn away.

As if he didn't want to be seen. As if he were displeased at her for looking, and with himself for letting her look. It happened so fast that Liv wondered if she'd imagined the irritation on his face. Maybe he was just grumpy because the fancy toilets in first class were full.

If her senses hadn't been heightened by self-consciousness, she might not have taken in that the man was of medium age, height and build, with wavy brown hair pushed away from a pale face punctuated with a mustache. His dress shirt, slacks and silk tie were in neutral colors, quietly expensive.

Liv replaced the magazine and looked across the aisle. Why worry about it? When the man came out, he would look away if he didn't want to be seen.

A click was followed by the folding of the thin door, and from the compact space emerged a completely different person. Gone was the mustache, and a tanned face matched tanned arms and legs, newly revealed by a short-sleeved, crewneck cotton shirt tucked into khaki shorts, accompanied by well-worn Tevas.

Straight, lighter hair was parted on one side and gelled into place. One hand carried a rolled-up safari hat, while the other steadied a soft leather case suspended on a worn shoulder strap—identical to the case the first man had carried in.

Liv couldn't decide which to believe: that the man could have pulled off the transformation, or that he had left and someone else entered the restroom right in front of her unseeing eyes. Well, men were quick. Maybe Dark Hair had finished, and Light Hair had slipped in, all during the time she'd had her nose buried in the magazine. Possible.

Light Hair turned and reentered first class, and Liv made her way to the restroom. Bright lights and a deafening exhaust fan popped on as she slid the lock into place. Nothing looked peculiar. If there had been any evidence, he would have it with him in his travel case.

Liv's eyes scanned the pocket-sized stainless steel sink bowl— wiped perfectly dry. Certainly more tidying-up than you'd expect of the average passenger. No, wait. A few medium-brown beads of water clung to the metal behind the faucet. Liv checked the mirror. Spotless in the center, but at the corners, more medium brown.

So he could have had light, naturally straight hair that a quick rinse had revealed. It would be easy to put instant fake tan on his face, with arms and legs already darkened beneath his long pants and sleeves. Stuff clothes into the leather case, and, presto, you're someone else. But what would the flight attendants and other passengers say?

Letting curiosity override caution, Liv folded open the door, stepped out and parted the first class curtains just an inch. There he was, two rows ahead, slouched in an aisle seat, with the safari hat covering his face. Pretending to be asleep. If the attendants thought he was sleeping through the rest of the flight, they might forget hours later what he had looked like before.

The other passengers paid no attention to him except for one, a strikingly handsome, fortyish man on the opposite side of the aisle. While Liv watched, Handsome Man rose from his seat, took an airline blanket and reached down to cover the sleeping Dark Hair-Light Hair. They must know each other. Was Handsome Man that caring, or was he covering up his friend's new look?

Liv retreated and pulled the curtains closed. There wasn't anything illegal about a person changing his appearance, and she had no solid proof he'd done it—just some brown drops in a restroom.

It didn't sound so bad when she described the incident to Anthony and Cal, striving to keep her voice lower than the in-flight movie the boys were watching.

"Sis, there's nothing wrong with changing into shorts and putting fake tan on your face," said Anthony.

"What about the hair dye?"

"Maybe he tried it and didn't like it."

Liv wasn't convinced. But if the boys weren't worried about the stranger, maybe she shouldn't be, either.

Dinner concluded with tong-equipped flight attendants doling out steaming lemon-scented towels from piles on a service cart. The in-flight movies were over now. Screens went blank and passengers pulled off headphones. They had been fed, scrubbed and entertained. It was time to settle down and have some quiet in the last few hours of darkness as their jet shot eastward to chase an early sunrise.

Anna, who'd perked up just enough to eat the light supper Mrs. Wescott had packed for her, had dozed through the light and noises of the early evening.

The dimming of the cabin lights for "night" created a hush among the passengers, and Anna's eyes popped open. She was ready for action, and she reached into the aisle toward Liv.

Holding Anna would mean walking her, and Liv wanted a nap just now. Besides, though she'd put the restroom stranger out of her mind for awhile, the possibility of seeing him again wasn't appealing. She'd recruit Cal for babysitting duty.

Liv leaned over Anthony and tapped Cal's shoulder. "Wake up—time to switch seats." Cal was propped against the window, eyes closed.

"Too late. I'm asleep."

"No, you're not. You're talking to me."

"I'm talking in my sleep."

Anthony, in the middle, closed his book, sighed and switched off his reading light. He clicked open his seat belt, looked from Cal to Liv and back to Cal, waiting.

Anna held out her arms and said, "Ca." She had elected her babysitter for the first shift. Cal crawled over Anthony and stood in the aisle, taking Anna from Mrs. Wescott and waiting for

Anthony to scoot to the window spot.

"If you can keep her happy for a little while, we'll each take a turn after you—won't we, Anthony?" Liv snuggled into the middle seat and closed her eyes.

Cal had a good relationship with Anna—she adored him, and Cal enjoyed playing with her most of the time, like the little sister he'd never had. But she looked fussy right now, and Cal was at a loss.

He beckoned to Mrs. Wescott for the diaper bag, unzipped it, and began to rate the contents. Disposable diapers, baby wipes, extra clothes—boring. Monkeys on a chain, teething ring, soft ladybug—better. Anna eyed his every move.

He found a plastic snack bag and held it out to her. Anna watched. She's considering things, just like her brother, Cal thought. She'll be a lot like Anthony when she grows up. That pleased him. A female version of his best friend.

The food didn't seem appealing to Cal: some health-food store cereal stuff, dried fruit, banana chips, tofu cubes. He couldn't blame Anna for just wanting to look and not eat. He tapped Liv with the bag and held it out. "What do we have here, big sister?"

Liv roused long enough to point out spirulina chunks, yogurt pretzels and carob balls. "The colored circles are Frootie Rings—juice-flavored cereal." Cal wrinkled his nose and hoped Anna wouldn't want any. He had a sensitive stomach.

He held Anna's index finger and guided it to touch bits of food through the plastic, calling out the colors of the cereal circles: "Green, blue, yellow, orange, pink, purple."

Anna tried: "Ee, oo, ell, aw, puh."

Cal began to chant, "Spirulina, pret-zel, rai-sin, carob ball, Frootie Rin-n-g!" He let his voice trail off. An "Unh, unh" from Anna let him know that he needed to do it again. Over and over and over again.

Ten minutes and a hundred repetitions later, Cal wondered if the other passengers were ready to murder him. Anna signaled she'd had enough by grabbing the plastic bag and lobbing it over the back of the seat. Cal cringed and called out, "Sorry!"

Now what? He plugged in his headphones and surfed channels till he found soothing classical music, putting the set on Anna's head. Her eyes grew wide and her brow furrowed in concentration. Cal congratulated himself on a brilliant idea and sat back to enjoy the results.

Just enough sound leaked from the loose-fitting headphones for him to hear the beat, and he swung Anna back and forth to it. He felt her relax, and her drooping eyelids made him sleepy, too. When her foot struck the volume control and sent a blast through the earpieces, Anna squealed and started to cry. Cal pulled the plug.

"I didn't do it!"

The crying stopped, but her lower lip puckered.

Cal looked up and down the darkened aisle. He could walk a few laps, then pass her off to Liv or Anthony. She might fall asleep before his turn came again.

"Let's get away from the evil headphones." He replaced the sippy cup in the diaper bag and stood. It felt good to stretch. Jiggling Anna and patting her back, Cal made his way down the aisle to the rear of the plane, turned and reversed his steps.

He walked to the curtains separating First Class from the rest of the cabin and began a slow about-face, but stopped when a chubby hand shot out and pulled a curtain panel, creating a small gap. "No, we don't go in there," he whispered. "Here, let's put it back."

Cal positioned Anna's hand on his arm so she could "help." Reaching up to shift the drape, he caught sight of a familiar profile and nearly collapsed on rubbery knees. Dozing in first class, looking completely at home in the twenty-first century, was the pirate Robert Francis Morehouse.

Chapter Six

Technically, of course, Morehouse was no longer a pirate. He was a somewhat-legal antiques dealer, transported to the present after a four-year stint in the early twentieth century. Cal and Anthony had traveled to St. Augustine, 1777, where they met Morehouse and he proceeded to kidnap them. Their escape had been complicated by his holding on and time-traveling with them.

The story should have ended when the boys dropped in to check on Morehouse and found themselves between the former pirate and a killer. They'd all risked their lives to save each other, and the end result was that Morehouse was now loose in the twenty-first century. Cal and Anthony had kept from Liv the fact that they'd made one last trip—ten years into the future—and found Morehouse flourishing.

Even now he seemed to be functioning amazingly well— he'd only been in the modern world about six months. If he saw Morehouse now, Cal wasn't supposed to know about some shady business deals, or Morehouse's metamorphosis from crook to charter fishing boat captain to golf course owner.

Morehouse's character had seemed pretty solid to Cal and Anthony on their visit to the future, but the man sitting four rows in front of him was not so mellow. Could it mean danger for them? Anna sensed the tension in Cal's body and clung to him. Cal replaced the curtain silently and returned to his seat to tell Anthony and Liv this latest development.

"Wakee, wakee," warbled a flight attendant through the intercom. Two of her co-workers began a stop-and-go trip down the aisle with a rolling cart full of beverages, efficiently passing coffee, tea, juices and water to sleepy passengers.

The warbler's co-worker swept along the aisle in a second wave, offering danishes and cereal with milk. Bringing up the rear guard was a young man who distributed plastic platters of scrambled eggs, link sausages and toast. The smells and sounds brought the cabin to life.

Liv and Cal took single servings of everything while Anthony took doubles, part of his continuing effort to gain weight that never appeared.

Cal yawned and stared at his tray. "You realize it's actually three o'clock in the morning, don't you? I don't think I can do sausage in the middle of the night." Before Liv could answer, a fork snaked under Cal's right arm, speared his sausage, and disappeared. Anthony chewed and swallowed with a satisfied nod.

Liv pulled Cal's tray closer to hers and shooed Anthony's fork away just as it came in and hovered over Cal's egg. "Keep talking like that, and you'll have nothing left to eat. Where we're going, it's already eight in the morning and lunch is going to be your next meal. Just think of this as a morning that came fast."

Now that people were stirring, Liv wanted to make her way forward and get a better look at Robert Morehouse. From what the boys had told her, an unexpected meeting with him might be awkward, and Liv couldn't help them avoid Morehouse unless she knew what he looked like.

There was a chance of bumping into Light Hair again, but she'd have to risk it. Her gut told her the connection between the two men hadn't been her imagination, and if Handsome was really Morehouse, the whole thing could turn into something she didn't want her parents to see. They knew nothing of the box or time travel adventures.

The food and beverage trolleys retired, and passengers chowed down. Another minute and they'd be expecting drink refills and making trips to the restroom. Time to make a move.

Liv cut her eyes to Cal and Anthony, and nodded her head in the direction of first class. They returned the nod and continued eating.

She passed a service area, where the flight attendants were busy refilling coffee carafes, chatting about where they would go and what they would do in London. It was now or never. She took a deep breath and opened the curtain.

No one paid attention to her. Liv stood in the aisle and waited for Handsome Man to turn his head. Somehow she knew she would see the details Cal had told her to watch for: a little gray around the temples in the rich black hair, piercing blue eyes, and a muscular body. A fine-looking face marred by one long scar snaking across the right cheekbone.

Her breath caught in her throat as the man turned his head toward the First Class attendant, who rushed to refill his orange juice glass, flashing him a smile of perfectly bleached teeth. It was Morehouse, all right, and he was dazzling the attendant with his pirate charm. The young woman's face flushed and her hand trembled as she poured the juice.

Light Hair was watching the scene, a bemused smile on his face. That was good. It kept him facing forward and diverted his attention from Liv. All she had to do was turn around and sneak back to her seat.

Morehouse must have said something witty. The attendant giggled, looked up self-consciously, and noticed Liv.

Perhaps she mistook Liv's look of surprise at being caught staring for something else. Disapproval? Nosiness? Whatever is was, a frown wrinkled her lovely brow, and she walked purposefully toward Liv.

"I'm sorry, Miss, you shouldn't be here. If you need

something, just ask Lorinda or Jill." She pointed a manicured fingernail toward the coach section.

Lancelot Cumpston turned his head in the direction of the pretty attendant's stern gaze and grimaced when he saw Liv. That one again!

It probably didn't matter that she'd noticed him, but it was annoying. He prided himself on being nearly invisible, the most discreet partner in the very discreet antiques firm of Cumpston, Pridgeon and McKnickel.

Not every sale required secrecy, but when customers dealt with CP&M, discretion was an expected part of the service. Only those in an elite inner circle might know someone who knew someone who could contact one of the partners to procure antiques and rare objects that no regular dealer would touch.

McKnickel was the antiques expert who had founded the firm. He'd engaged in questionable practices, exaggerating the age and worth of his merchandise and making a modest profit. But when Cumpston and his friend, Carmine Pridgeon, had come on board, business had skyrocketed. Pridgeon made millions for the firm in illegal real estate dealings, and Cumpston, who was absolutely ruthless, went by the philosophy that all laws were made to be broken. His was now the name that came first, though the company logo couldn't be found on any sign, stationery or telephone listing.

Everything had been fine until Pridgeon suggested bringing his new acquaintance, Morehouse, into the mix. The man attracted attention wherever he went.

Maybe he was worth it. He took advantage of customers and other dealers with ease, but was almost impossible to fool—a valuable combination. His encyclopedic knowledge of antiques was almost eerie. It was as if he'd been there when the pieces were new. He could talk wealthy clients into buying expensive objects they never knew they wanted. Rich ladies swooned over him, while he charmed their husbands into opening their checkbooks. He closed deals and made the buyers happy to part with their cash.

But when some of your inventory was stolen or fake, it was risky to be memorable, and being memorable was part of Morehouse's style. If he knew just how far outside the law Cumpston, Pridgeon and McKnickel operated, he'd be a lot more careful.

In fact, he might not even want to do business with them. Maybe it was time for them to part ways with Morehouse, before he learned too much and became a liability they would need to dispose of.

It might be best to let Morehouse phase out gradually. They had an important delivery to make next month, to an Australian collector. They'd take the firm's private jet, and if Morehouse put up a fuss, they could stuff him in a packing crate and dump him in the ocean on the way back.

Cumpston's coffee was cold, and the attendant wasn't attending to it. The ridiculous girl was still simpering over Morehouse. Cumpston frowned, pushed the call button, and held it.

Liv's cheeks burned as she made her way back to her seat, grateful that her parents were too busy filling out landing cards to notice her. She was worried, not embarrassed. Morehouse had never looked in her direction, but Light Hair's motionless stare had been unnerving.

"It's your guy, all right." She buckled her seat belt and removed Anthony's glass of orange juice from his hand, draining it in one swallow. "He was too busy flirting with the flight attendant to notice me, but his creepy friend did."

Anthony frowned at his empty glass and took it back. "Cal and I talked while you were gone. With any luck, we'll never cross paths with Morehouse in Customs or Baggage Claim, but if we do, we'll make the best of it and greet him calmly."

Anthony ran his hand through his dark hair, which usually stood up in spikes but was flat from hours of being squashed by an airline pillow. "As for the other guy, we don't know him and don't want to meet him. Avoiding eye contact seems like the way to go."

Liv turned to Cal, who had stared out the window during the conversation. The ball of his foot was planted firmly on the floor, and his heel nervously bounced up and down, powering a leg that jiggled as if attached to a vibrator. His color wasn't good, and he didn't look up to making the best of anything. She hoped he could manage the avoiding eye contact part.

She tried to sound upbeat for Cal's sake. "Let's don't make things worse by worrying about them. To tell you the truth, I'm relieved to see your pirate traveling on a plane, looking normal. It's the first sign we've had that he may turn out okay."

She paused, waiting for Cal or Anthony to agree with her, and the silence stretched into several seconds. Cal continued to look out the window while Anthony studied his orange juice glass.

Liv crossed her arms, then her legs. She twisted her mouth and nodded slowly, as if talking to herself. "You visited him again, didn't you? And if you didn't tell me about it, there must be a reason. What didn't you want me to know?"

"It's not like that, Sis," Anthony said in a low tone. "Morehouse turned, uh—turns—out great. It's just that. . ." Anthony hung his head in embarrassment. "When we parted company in St. Augustine, his last words to us were to stop playing around with time travel. I'm sure he thinks we honored that request."

Liv uncrossed her arms and studied her brother's face. "And now you're worried that if you run into him, he'll ask you if you've followed his advice. You think he might see through you if you try to lie, since neither one of you is very good at it." She arched an eyebrow and waited.

Anthony and Cal quickly filled her in on what Morehouse had told them when they'd encountered him ten years into the future, as he'd briefly described his progression from unscrupulous antiques dealer to charter fishing boat captain to miniature golf course owner and happily married man.

Liv chewed her lip. "I hate to admit it, but I'm glad you sneaked into the future. He's going to be fine on his own."

Cal's knee stopped pumping. "You're right! It's going to be okay, unless we mess it up by letting him know we've seen him and make him do something different than he would have done, but we won't do that, will we, I mean, I won't, will I? You two may have nerves of steel, but I—"

"Shut up, Cal," Liv and Anthony hissed together. Anthony gripped his friend's arm at the elbow and leaned in close.

"If we run into Morehouse, you are not allowed to speak on your own. If he recognizes us and says something, you are allowed to smile and nod, and you get to say one word. Take your choice between 'Hi' and 'Hello.' That's it. You do not ask him how he is. You do not say goodbye." Anthony let go of Cal's arm. "You let me do the talking. Period."

Instead of taking offense, Cal looked relieved. He nodded and smiled weakly.

"Perfect—just like that," said Liv.

Chapter Seven

"Welcome to Gatwick Airport and the United Kingdom." A dignified man stamped the passports of the Wescott traveling group, then peered over his spectacles at baby Anna and smiled. "And especially you, young lady," he said, pointing at her and raising the pitch of his voice. "Anything to declare?"

Anna returned his smile and reached out to him, stuffed bunny in hand.

"One bunny rabbit, thank you, Miss. Enjoy your stay." He pretended to examine it, then nodded and turned to Mr. and Mrs. Wescott. "And how about the rest of her lovely family?" The grownups completed the formalities while Liv, Anthony and Cal tried to look around without appearing to look around.

"I see him." Liv kept her voice low and pointed in the opposite direction, as if studying something interesting. "On Cal's right at three o'clock. Don't turn and look. He's picking up his carry-on bag and heading for the escalator to Baggage Claim. His friend is just finishing at the desk next to him." She turned around to face the boys so her back would be to both men as they passed by. Cal and Anthony did the same, and the three stood silently.

"Wow, standing like statues in the middle of a noisy crowd—what a brilliant way to blend," muttered Anthony. He nodded his head and laughed, as if appreciating a joke. "Let's try not to attract attention for looking seriously weird."

"Good advice, Bro," said Liv, slipping her arms into the straps of her backpack and reaching down to get Anna's diaper bag. She poked her finger into Cal's shoulder and whispered, "Nothing to worry about. Anthony does the talking. Remember."

At the baggage carousels, first class and coach passengers could mingle at last, and Cumpston didn't like it a bit. They wouldn't be rubbing shoulders with anyone if the firm's private jet hadn't been undergoing needed repairs. They'd have landed at a special terminal, zipped through Customs and been on their way. Even on a commercial flight, if he were traveling alone, Cumpston would have walked halfway to the trains by now, with no checked baggage.

But Morehouse had his own way of doing things. He had to be charming, which involved not only clothes for every occasion, but gifts for clients, tucked into the extra luggage.

So they had to wait. Cumpston hated waiting.

He couldn't be bothered with being charming, either. Make someone mad? Double-cross a client? It wasn't usually a problem. He could disguise himself and seem to disappear, like a chameleon. And it didn't take a suitcase that had to be checked and waited for at the carousel, either.

His sour mood wasn't helped by spotting the bratty young girl who had dared to look at him, along with her too-perfect suburban family, complete with bouncing baby sister. They were on the opposite side of the carousel, utterly unaware of his presence, he was certain.

Amazing how ordinary people went through most of their lives unaware. If confronted directly by someone with superior intelligence like himself, they occasionally had a moment of insight, a moment of fear, when they realized how vulnerable they were. But usually they were like sheep, there for fleecing. Only those who got in his way posed a problem.

Cumpston's annoyance turned to concern as he watched Morehouse stride around the curve of the carousel to retrieve his suitcase right in front of the sheep family, then do a classic double-take as he passed the two boys standing with the girl.

"Well, blow me down, it's—it's—" spluttered Morehouse.

"That's right, it's us," Anthony cut in, keeping his voice low and his eyes on his parents, who were focused on waiting for their first piece of luggage.

Morehouse followed his gaze. "Ahh, I see. Mum and Dad know nothing of your grand adventures, and you'd like to keep it that way. I'm all for that myself." He glanced over his shoulder at Cumpston, who made a point of checking his watch and ignoring Morehouse. "My associate likes to keep a low profile."

Morehouse jumped forward and lifted an expensive-looking brown leather suitcase from the carousel's conveyor belt. Instead of making his way toward his partner, he came back. He raised an eyebrow at Liv and turned to the boys.

"It's okay, she knows," said Anthony.

"It's only okay if you've stopped doing it," replied Morehouse. He narrowed his eyes at Cal, who was following orders and being quiet.

He continued, "With apologies for my abruptness, I must be off. It's good to see you—enjoy your stay in London. It's my city and I missed it during my years of exile, but I find I'm homesick for Florida. Can you believe it?" Cal nodded vigorously and Morehouse gave him a peculiar look. "Business is good—I'm traveling the world and making more money than ever before, but I may go back to the States and find completely honest work—hire on with a charter fishing fleet or something."

Cal avoided Morehouse's piercing gaze and glanced across the room at Cumpston. A look of disgust beamed from Cumpston's eyes and focused on Liv. Cal's fear for her won out over his resolve to be quiet.

"Good plan!" he blurted. "Time to get in with a better crowd!"

Liv stared at Cal while Anthony mouthed *shut up* silently. But the floodgates were open, and Cal babbled on in his attempt to place all possible distance between the Wescotts and Morehouse's alarming friend.

"I bet you'd like the fishing business. You'd be good at it. Who knows—you might even meet a nice lady and settle down—find something else, like a miniature golf course." Anthony cringed and grabbed Cal's arm, squeezing with his fingers until Cal winced.

"Well," replied the startled Morehouse, "I don't know about that, but perhaps you're right." He reached into the back pocket of his stylishly casual linen slacks and pulled a business card from his wallet.

"But my present 'crowd', as you put it, is the esteemed firm of Cumpston, Pridgeon and McKnickel, highly successful dealers of antiques in Portobello Road. That's Lance Cumpston over there, looking grumpy." He pressed the card into Cal's hand and smiled. It read simply, Robert F. Morehouse, Antiques and Collectibles, followed by a mobile phone number.

Morehouse sighed and repocketed his wallet. "I assume you're guessing about my marginally legal activities because you know about my past, and you've reached an accurate conclusion." The shadow of a smile passed across his face.

"I meant to reform—I really did, but it's just so easy to make a fortune if you don't mind breaking a few laws. And I'm good at it!" He shrugged at Liv's frown. "But it's time for this old pirate to clean up his life." He grinned at Anthony and Cal. "After all, I can't keep relying on you two to transport me from era to era for fresh starts. I was thinking about cutting ties with those three in a few months, after I finish all the deals I've started. But maybe I'll go ahead and break off now."

Liv spoke for the first time. "Mr. Morehouse, I have a bad feeling about your partner over there, but I think we've interfered with your personal life quite enough." She raised her eyebrows at Cal and stopped short of telling Morehouse that Cal had just revealed his future to him. "Maybe you shouldn't alter your plans too much—I think you need to be very careful around Mr. Cumpston."

Morehouse gave Liv an approving nod. "Incredibly perceptive of you, my dear. I let myself get careless in St. Augustine with an inept rascal named Abernathy, and it almost got me killed." He lowered his voice to barely a whisper. "You don't let yourself get careless around Cumpston. That will get you killed, slowly and painfully. There've been rumors..."

Liv pressed her lips together and twisted them, wondering if Morehouse knew that she had caught his partner's attention on the plane. Now Cumpston was watching her talk to Morehouse. Would he feel threatened?

She was ready to commandeer a swift goodbye. She pulled at Anthony's arm. "Dad's going to want some help with the luggage, guys. We'd better go." To Morehouse, she said, "It was nice to meet you. Good luck."

Anthony smiled and said, "See you around." Cal looked at the floor.

"Is there something you need to tell me?" Morehouse's tone was firm but kind.

Cal replied, "It's just. . ." He shrugged. "It's your partner—I hope we didn't look at him too much." He nodded his head toward Liv. "Especially her."

"Oh, I wouldn't worry. But Cumpston can be a dangerous man when he chooses, and I'm impressed that you sensed it. Listen to your instincts and stay away from him." The three watched him catch up with his tanned partner, who was walking swiftly toward the escalator, as if trying to make it hard for Morehouse to keep up.

"I don't like it," whispered Cal as they made their way back to Mr. and Mrs. Wescott. The entire exchange had taken less than five minutes, and the Wescotts had been watching for their bags on the carousel, too busy to notice the interaction between the children and the handsome stranger.

"Morehouse is right," said Anthony. "There's nothing to worry about. We'll probably never see them again."

"Dad's waving at us," said Liv. "The luggage is here." They walked back to the carousel and quickly formed a suitcase-passing brigade.

From the escalator, Cumpston eyed the three of them. The girl acted like she was in charge—that made her more dangerous than the boys. Why had she watched him, and how did she know Morehouse? There was so much about Morehouse he didn't know, and unknowns were risks. It was important to eliminate risks.

Chapter Eight

"The Gatwick Express will take us straight to Victoria Station."

Mr. Wescott threaded the luggage cart through the tapestry of humanity and parked it where his wife could lean on it and balance Anna. Liv, Anthony and Cal watched him make his way to the train ticket counter and resumed their argument, discreetly standing just out of Mrs. Wescott's hearing.

"Stop worrying, Sis." Anthony fidgeted, shifting his jacket and carry-on bag from one hand to the other. "Morehouse turns out fine—we already know that."

"That's how it was without your talking to him about his future. It's different now. Maybe he's on edge, maybe he's realizing he needs to get out in a hurry. What if he doesn't act the same around his partners and they get in a fight or something?" She tried to keep her expression neutral, but she knew the strain showed in her voice.

Cal pointed ahead. "Chances are, nothing will come from anything we've seen or said. Meanwhile, let's have some fun. I've never been on a train before!"

Liv smiled in spite of herself and fell into step behind her parents. She marveled at the number of trains and tracks, waiting in the darkness to absorb the stream of passengers flowing from the terminal. People darted around the enormous garage, all seeming to know where they were going. Her parents conferred, heads close together, and her mother nodded and pointed to an empty car on an empty train.

The fluorescent lighting cast a blue sheen onto the plush seats, beckoning passengers to climb in and plop down in quiet comfort. Liv felt drained. She was ready to speed to London, far away from pirates.

They boarded the car and took turns shoving their suitcases into the luggage hold. She slid into one of four seats, two forward and two backward, with a table between them. The boys joined her, piling backpacks into the fourth seat. She caught sight of her reflection in the window and saw a face that looked pinched and pale.

The train pulled out of the station. The vibration and noise made it easier to let conversation go and enjoy the ride, while they all sipped on bottles of juice purchased from the food trolley. Early morning light crept into the train, competing with the interior lights and revealing the English landscape. A field with grazing sheep. A town with charming tile-roofed houses clustered together, a modern supermarket and parking lot, a station with passengers standing, waiting for their train to stop.

They were really in a foreign country. Anna and her parents dozed on the other side of the aisle, but Liv, Anthony and Cal stared out the window, taking everything in.

In the first class car of the train, Cumpston found the ride barely tolerable. The scenery was nondescript, the company of Morehouse annoying, and the presence of so many people in first class was starting to smother him. What was the point of paying extra for something if others could have it, too? He needed to think, and who could think with inconsiderate idiots yakking on phones ("Hullo, it's me. I'm on the train.") and rattling newspapers?

And there sat Morehouse, unperturbed, with the maddening expression of good-humor Cumpston had often observed on attractive people. Pleased with themselves, that's what they were, because the world always went their way. People smiled at them at every turn, wanted to do things for them, wanted to make life easy for them. A handsome man like Morehouse wouldn't know what it was like to have to claw your way from the bottom and fight for every pound you made.

Now, the reason for his current worries was sitting in the seat across from him, half-smiling, gathering admiring glances like a dog might gather ticks on a walk through the woods.

That made Morehouse a magnet for trouble. People noticed him—they remembered him. It had been a mistake to involve him so closely in the antiques side of their business. The internet and real estate scams of Cumpston, Pridgeon, and McKnickel were more sensitive and dangerous, and Morehouse was the nosy type who might want a piece of the action, which he didn't deserve.

He needed to be dealt with. How and when could be decided later. The other issue must be addressed right now.

"So tell me, Morehouse, how do you know those delightful children?" The sneer on his face crept into his voice. "Relatives, perhaps?"

"Oh, no, just...friends—acquaintances, actually." Morehouse sounded confident and unconcerned, but he had missed a beat when he answered, tripping Cumpston's internal alarm.

"Hmm. . ." Cumpston reached for a copy of the *Times* and opened it, more to hide his face than to search for something to read. The family would get off the train at Victoria Station. Perhaps they needed watching for a bit.

The Gatwick Express eased into the western side of Victoria Station and slid to a smooth stop. Morehouse had expected Cumpston to spring out of his seat, grab his luggage, and exit swiftly, but instead he continued to read his newspaper. After a full two minutes, Cumpston rose slowly and folded the paper, leaving it on the table. He removed his leather case from beneath his seat, then dismounted the train, never so much as looking at Morehouse to see if he were following.

Morehouse didn't like Cumpston, didn't want him as a friend, but the sudden chill in his manner was troubling. He followed him down the train steps, and watched as his partner scanned the area and moved forward. Morehouse caught up and followed his line of sight. They were tailing the boys and their family.

Light poured through the vast transparent roof of Victoria Station's open area and bounced off the white terrazzo floor. Pigeons loitered and relaxed while people rushed past them.

The family, minus the father, stood by a money-changing kiosk, probably waiting for him to return from purchasing travel passes for the London tube and trains. They chatted happily and pointed to the stores above the concourse, the shop fronts, and building exteriors housed inside the huge structure, unaware that Cumpston was keeping an eye on them.

Morehouse grew more uneasy by the minute. What was Cumpston up to? Surely he didn't think these kids were a threat. He sighed. Cumpston's moods were unpredictable, his remarks often cryptic.

If he had a good side, Morehouse needed to get on it in a hurry. He tapped him on the shoulder. "Let me buy you a coffee. What do you like?" Morehouse indicated a nearby coffee shop and hoped he sounded friendly, but not too friendly. At ease, not trying too hard.

"What? Oh, all right then." Cumpston pointed with his briefcase toward the Terminus Place. "Meet me there, at the taxi stand." Morehouse stepped away and disturbed a gathering of pigeons, who flew over his head, politely restraining themselves until they passed Cumpston. Then they released two white bombs, spattering the carefully pressed T-shirt and causing its wearer to press his lips together and turn an unhealthy shade of red-purple.

Morehouse stole a look back and groaned silently. His companion's expression was murderous. He hoped the hatred was directed at the birds.

Chapter Nine

Six travelers and as many suitcases made their way to the front of the queue at the taxi stand. Mr. Wescott could be an indulgent parent at times, but he was a tyrant when it came to luggage. One piece of checked baggage per person, and if you couldn't tote it up a flight of stairs, you didn't need it. Even Anna carried her bunny rabbit in a teeny-tiny backpack.

Liv looked up and down the row of empty cabs and admired the orderliness of the system. Waiting passengers moved forward every ninety seconds or so, and cab drivers pulled their vehicles forward. The cab at the front swallowed up the passenger at the head of the queue and sped away. Very efficient and civilized.

She studied the parties waiting ahead of them: a couple holding hands and a slender man in a dark suit with matching dark turban. A pair of elderly ladies in plain skirts, cardigans and sensible shoes stood behind the Wescotts. The couple and the turbaned man barely gave their cabs time to put on the brakes before opening the doors and climbing in. Suddenly, it was the Wescotts' turn.

As they picked up their belongings and prepared to move to

their cab, Liv became aware of a young man in a leather jacket swaggering toward the cab that should have been theirs. The tattooed, shaved head, the piercings and skin-tight black jeans complemented his sneer.

Mr. Wescott raised his hand as if to protest, then looked back at his family and shook his head. Liv was sure her dad would have challenged the punk if he'd been traveling alone. The cab driver shrugged.

The queue-breaker opened the door and leaned down to enter his ill-gotten ride. A blue-veined hand clenched his arm and, catching him off-guard, spun him around, where he faced two very angry old ladies.

"You should be ashamed of yourself! Taking advantage of a nice family that way. And with a baby! What's the world coming to?" They pressed in fearlessly, like mongooses standing down a cobra. They had to be in their eighties, and the taller one's curly white head was barely higher than Liv's shoulder.

The cab poacher began to stutter an excuse, but was immediately shouted down by the shorter woman, who brandished her cane perilously close to his nose ring. "Didn't your mum teach you any manners? I wager it'd break her heart right in two if she could see you now."

The young man had clearly lost both battle and dignity, and he turned to leave the way he'd come. But the octogenarian avengers weren't through. "Oh, no, you don't! We won't have any of that, sneaking back to break the queue again after we're gone. All the way around to the end for you. That's right, step lively, that's better."

Their victory complete, they stepped back to wait their turn.

The queue burst into applause. The cab driver removed his cap and bowed to the women. The Wescott party stood frozen, watching, a little afraid to move.

The old lady with the cane pounded it impatiently on the sidewalk, and her friend shouted at Mr. Wescott, "Well, go on— don't just stand about. Get in! You're holding up the queue!"

"Nothing like a bit of drama to start your morning—welcome to London!" The driver secured the luggage, nodded at the address given to him, and merged the cab into the stream of traffic. "Beautiful day to be in London, right? But then that's always true for me. No sir, nowhere else I'd rather be—right here in the middle of things, driving my cab." Liv found his accent delightful. It sounded down-to-earth, friendly. He continued, "And what brings you folks to London—business or pleasure?"

Mr. Wescott inclined his head toward his family and Cal. "Pleasure for them—I'm afraid I'll be working most of the time." Liv noted that her father didn't reveal what kind of business. He was proud of his work, but he didn't like lawyer jokes, which strangers often felt astonishingly free to share when they learned he was an attorney.

The cabbie braked for a red light. "Well now, if you love your job half as much as I love mine, it won't be a burden to do it." The light changed to green, and he tapped his horn to encourage a car dawdling at the intersection.

"And if you hate it, at least you'll be doing it in the greatest city in the world." He left it at that, just short of asking what Mr. Wescott did for a living. The silence grew. Anthony filled in the gap. "Dad's a lawyer. He'll be working with a barrister here this summer." Mr. Wescott's smile never faltered, but Liv saw the muscles in the back of his neck tighten.

The cabbie glanced over his shoulder at Mr. Wescott. "Guess you've heard the old proverb about two farmers who each claimed to own the same cow, right? One pulled at the head, the other pulled at the tail, and the cow got milked by a solicitor." He threw back his head and laughed with his whole upper body, a guffaw that shook the front seat.

Noticing that no one was laughing, he peered in the rearview mirror and caught Mrs. Wescott's wide-eyed stare, then pulled his cap lower on his face. "That's the trouble with solicitor jokes," he grumbled. "Solicitors don't think they're funny, and nobody else thinks they're jokes."

This time, it was Mr. Wescott's turn to belly-laugh. The ice broken, he and the cabbie began to chat about the weather, the traffic and who was likely to win the World Cup. Mrs. Wescott's smile returned, and she pointed out sights to Anna and her bunny as they passed them. The driver gave them a history of London cabs, informing them that they'd been licensed since the year sixteen sixty-two and were still officially called hackney carriages.

The grownups continued to listen while Cal turned to Anthony. "Your dad's a lawyer, so what was that about solicitors? I thought those were people who sell stuff door-to-door..."

Anthony explained, "Solicitor is Britspeak for lawyer. American attorneys do any part of lawyering they want to. But if he practiced here, he'd have to choose between being a barrister or a solicitor."

"Solicitors go to trial," said Liv. "Barristers are considered a little higher up."

"But trial lawyers can make a lot of money!" said Cal.

Liv shrugged. "Go figure."

They turned their attention to the sights. Trafalgar Square was coming up, with its huge statues, lofty monument and hundreds of pigeons. Liv pointed them out to Anna and said, "The pigeons of Trafalgar Square—just like in the guidebook! Aren't they graceful?"

"Winged rats, is what I call 'em," opined the cabbie. "Now there's a bird that's useful." He pointed to a young man with a leather glove and sleeve, looking intently at the branches of a tall tree on the edge of the square. The handler gave a signal with his free hand, and a beautiful falcon glided from the highest branch, landing elegantly on his master's sleeved arm. Bystanders oohed their appreciation, as did Anthony and Cal, but Liv observed the cabbie frowning into his rearview mirror. He had done that twice in the last few minutes.

Mr. Wescott ignored the spectacle as well and checked his watch. He leaned toward the cabbie.

"We appreciate the tour, but wouldn't it be faster to go directly to our flat?" Liv recognized her dad's "I'm-being-polite-but-I'm-irritated" tone of voice. It was clear he thought the cabbie was trying to turn a short trip into a long one to charge a higher fare.

"Sorry, sir," replied the cabbie, his eyes darting from the traffic ahead to his rearview mirror and back. "It seemed a cab about three lengths back was following us, so I deviated a bit to see what would happen." The traffic light ahead turned red, and the cab glided to a stop. The cabbie held the steering wheel with one hand and rubbed his face with the other.

No one spoke. The light changed to green, and the cabbie drove forward. He turned left, waiting until the last second to use his turn signal so as not to give away his intentions. Seconds later, his lips came together in a thin line and the furrow of his brow deepened.

"Sir, d'ya know a fair-haired chap with an Aussie hat and a dark tan?" He spoke calmly, but the lighthearted tone was gone. Liv felt her heart pound in her chest. She glanced at the boys. They were perfectly still, listening.

Mr. Wescott replied, "I don't know anyone like that—it can't be related to us."

"I spotted him holding his cabbie's shoulder and pointing at us a couple of times." Concern creased his friendly face. "I hope you're not one of those solicitors who get in with a dangerous crowd."

Mr. Wescott's expression of concern matched the cabbie's. "I assure you, my business is boringly safe." He glanced around the cab's interior. "I'd never bring my family along if it weren't."

"All the same, I'm going to drive right on past your building without stopping. If I'm satisfied this bloke is nowhere to be seen, I'll circle the block and bring you round again." The cabbie drove the remaining half block to the intersection with his right turn signal on, then changed to left at the last second and turned that way.

The evasive maneuver was unneeded, though. The cab had dropped back.

Lance Cumpston was satisfied. He glanced in the cab's side view mirror and chuckled. There was the sheep family's cab, finally parked in front of the Asquith Gardens Apartments, children spilling out onto the sidewalk. He could find them if he chose to. He sat back in his seat and saw Morehouse studying him.

"You wouldn't be afraid to do what's necessary, would you, Robert?" Cumpston normally avoided real names in public places. Even in private, he addressed his associates by last name, but this was a crucial display of power. The new one needed to be put in his place.

But it seemed Morehouse could play that game, too. "Of course not, Lance."

Cumpston recoiled at the sound of his own name. Such disrespect. Who did he think he was? Who was he, really?

Morehouse leaned closer to Cumpston and spoke quietly. "You'll never have a problem with me over doing what's necessary. It's your preoccupation with the unnecessary that's attracting my attention."

He inclined his head toward the building where the Wescotts were now filing in, one at a time, and looked back at Cumpston. "Those are kids, Lance—no need to get paranoid over a bunch of children. So what if the girl figured out you changed your look on the plane—if she did."

He gripped Cumpston's forearm—another inappropriate informality, Cumpston noted. "What do you think she's going to do, Lance—hire a private investigator to run background checks on us?"

Cumpston's bronzed-from-the-bottle complexion changed as all traces of natural pink drained from his face. "No, no—of course not. Let's drop it, shall we?" He withdrew himself from Morehouse's grasp and sat back in the seat. Maybe worrying about the girl was a waste of time.

Morehouse, on the other hand...Morehouse was disrespectful—it just wouldn't do.

Chapter Ten

The exterior of the converted mansion that now housed Asquith Serviced Apartments oozed Englishness and past grandeur. The enormous hand-carved door looked as if it belonged in a cathedral. It opened without a creak into a marble-tiled foyer that still managed to look impressive, despite being broken up into an entryway, seating area, check-in desk and baggage hold.

The Wescott party checked in without incident. The slight, dark-eyed man staffing the desk seemed delighted to see them—his cinnamon-colored face was split by a wide smile that revealed dazzling white teeth. He completed the paperwork quickly and produced keycards for the adults.

The smile sagged as he looked up and down the hall, sighed, and pounded a bell on the desk with his fist. "My lazy brother-in-law is often nowhere to be found when baggage needs to go up, but I can assure you he will materialize at the end of your stay to take your bags down, hoping for a generous tip. Please give him none."

He snorted, raised the counter on its hinges, and came forward to reach for their luggage. "Allow me to assist you. Right this way." He ignored the ringing telephone.

Mr. Wescott gave a sympathetic shake of his head. "No need to leave your post when I have three able bodies right here. It seems you're already doing double duty as attendant and manager."

He grinned in appreciation and held up a travel brochure and tool belt. "Don't forget concierge and repairman." He pointed with the brochure to a corner in the hallway as he picked up the phone. "The lift's over there."

Mr. Wescott handed a keycard to Liv, and asked, "Can I put you three in charge of the rest of the luggage? We're on the third floor—number three-oh-five."

"Sure, Dad," Anthony said, gripping a suitcase in each hand and nodding at Cal to do the same. "We'll be waiting for you."

They made their way down a narrow passage to an elevator the size of a phone booth, with beautiful brass appointments, oriental carpet and gleaming wood trim. A glance told them the luggage and the three of them couldn't fit into the tiny space at the same time.

"Here," said Anthony, pushing ahead of Cal and motioning for him to hand over the additional suitcases. "I'll go on—you two take the stairs. Just close that collapsible brass gate, will you?"

"Where's the door?" asked Cal. "You don't want to see this thing going between floors." He shuddered.

"Don't worry—I can close my eyes if I need to." Anthony held his finger at the button. "I'll give you a head start. See you on the third floor. Last one up has to unload all the luggage."

Cal turned and sprinted to the spiral staircase. "Don't push the button till I hit the first step!"

Liv watched him take the stairs two at a time and climb round and round. She followed, enjoying the pull of the steps on her leg muscles and feeling strong. "Up to two, up to two," chanted Cal ahead of her, passing a closed door that appeared to lead off to a hallway. "Up to three, up to three," he panted, stopping at the next landing and heading down the hall to look at apartment doors.

Liv knew the brass numbers would read two-oh-three, two-oh-four and two-oh-five, so why was Cal stopping here? She looked toward the elevator shaft. Here came Anthony, staring at Cal while the little cage passed the floor and continued its ascent. Brother and sister shrugged at each other as Cal raced back up the hall and tore into the stairs again, barely catching up with Liv at the end. The elevator was emptied of luggage, and Anthony said, "Sit down and catch your breath. We'll carry everything to the apartment."

Liv jumped in to be sure Cal understood his mistake. "Guess you didn't realize the lobby is the ground floor. After that, you start counting first and so on. The third floor is actually the fourth story."

"And I was supposed to know that how?" Cal grumbled. "I don't like being outsmarted by a building."

Liv picked up two suitcases and congratulated herself for choosing not to invite a friend on this trip. Friends could be high-maintenance.

It didn't take long for the efficient Mrs. Wescott to get everyone on task, settling into the apartment and unpacking while she worked on a grocery list. Sleeping assignments were made: grownups and Anna in the large bedroom, Liv in the second one, about the size of a walk-in closet, with the boys sleeping on the pullout sofa in the sitting room. Anthony and Cal slid their suitcases under the end tables flanking the sofa. The three agreed that Liv should keep the box in her room for now.

"If we each take ten minutes to freshen up in the bathroom," Mrs. Wescott instructed them, "we can hit the pavement, ready to sightsee, in under an hour. We'll pick up groceries on the way back."

"Ten minutes?" asked Anthony, sniffing his armpits. "What do I need to do that will take a whole ten minutes?"

Mrs. Wescott handed him a bar of soap and pointed to the bathroom. "Come out clean."

Chapter Eleven

Liv finished brushing her teeth and looked up, where her reflection in the mirror met her gaze with customary directness. Her curly, dark hair, pulled back into its usual ponytail, was just beginning to frizz in the humidity of an unair-conditioned London summer. Her blue eyes might have been more striking with makeup, though Liv couldn't imagine bothering. Her build was slim but solid from years of soccer and running and her nails would always be trimmed short, because the piano was a love she intended never to be without.

Hmm. . . A piano. Soccer. Running. She'd gone without any of them for more than a day, and she was feeling withdrawal. Not much she could do about the first two, but maybe she could convince her parents to let her take a run somewhere. There was a park visible from the huge windows of their sitting room. It would be fun to explore.

The street and neighborhood looked like a scene from Mary Poppins, and the flat itself was like a movie set with its high ceilings, elaborate plaster moldings and chandeliers. A ringing phone interrupted her reverie.

Brring-brring. Pause. Brring-brring. Pause. Even the sound of the phone was charming.

Through the inch-plus gap under the bathroom door, Liv could hear her mother say, "Hello?" then, "Oh, hello, Mrs. Havard! How thoughtful of you to call."

Liv emerged from the bathroom and crossed the navy and cream print carpet to stand by her mother and listen.

"Well, yes, we'd love to come by and meet you. Let me just get a pen and write the directions."

Her mother hung up and announced, "We're invited for tea."

"Great—I'm ready. Maybe I can practice on their piano for a few minutes and still have time to find a place to run when we get back."

Anthony was slouching on the sofa while Cal slept, stretched out on the floor beside him. He leaped over his friend and bounded to his sister's side.

"I'm sure Mrs. Havard isn't expecting all six of us, dear—she mentioned only Liv and me. But I guess you boys could come along if you like. They have a daughter a couple of years older than you. It should be fun for all of you to meet, and we can sightsee tomorrow. Maybe your father will want to rest—he has to work tomorrow." She looked around the room, then put her finger to her lips and followed the sound of snoring that drifted in from the bedroom. She tiptoed in and came out smiling.

"They're passed out on the bed. I put a blanket over them, and I'll tape a note to the doorframe explaining where we are and what to feed Anna."

The walk to the Underground station was fun, except for a silly thing that kept getting on Liv's nerves. The buildings were quaint, the shops were interesting and the people-watching was fantastic, but Anthony and Cal kept irritating her by poking and pinching each other, saying, "Hey—we're really in London!"

Why did it make her feel left out? Her parents had offered to let her invite a friend. She'd chosen not to.

She put it from her mind and walked beside her mother,

past planters overflowing with greenery to fat white columns that marked the entrance to the station, which was filled with vendors. Beyond them were the turnstiles, and Liv tried her pass first. The machine ate the ticket and instantly spat it out on the other side of the turnstile, which opened for her as a red light changed to green. She was in.

The others did the same, and after a couple of false starts, followed by a quick consultation of a wall map, they were on the proper platform waiting for their train.

There had been plenty to watch on the way down. Small billboards advertising shows in the theater district, a saxophonist playing jazz, his case open and filling up with coins and bills. Purposeful-looking grownups, on their way to very important places.

And kids her own age or a little older, hanging out and traveling with their friends, laughing and talking, calling other friends on cell phones.

In the relative quiet of the platform, she looked at her brother and his best friend again, sitting together on the bench, joking, enjoying each other's company. For the first time, she confronted the real reason she'd turned down her parents' offer to let her invite a friend on this trip.

Popular and outgoing, she had always assumed she could have a friend any time she wanted—the time had just never been right. And when the trip had come up, she'd been too engrossed in her own problems to find one in a hurry. At least, that had been her excuse. In fact, she wasn't sure she could do it.

What was the matter with her? She'd made friends quickly with Emily, a girl she'd met on a time travel trip to 1897. But the contact was short-lived, she reminded herself. She didn't have to nurture the relationship by spending lots of time on it, the way Anthony and Cal spent so much time together. Maybe she was too selfish to have a friend.

On the other hand, maybe she could practice making a friend with the Havards' daughter. How hard could it be? They'd probably have a lot in common—music, for instance—and it would be easy to arrange to spend time together, with Liv going over most days to practice on the family's piano. Suddenly, the world didn't look so lonely.

When their train sped up to the platform and stopped, a recorded male voice boomed, "Mind the gap, mind the gap," meaning the space between the train and platform, and the four of them scrambled on after the rush of departing passengers cleared away.

They settled into their seats as the train pulled away from the platform. A refined, velvety female voice took over the announcement chores and Anthony closed his eyes, sighing at the way she said, "Sloane Square." Cal shook his head at him and made gagging noises.

But their goofiness wasn't annoying her so much now. Friends could have fun together being silly, she told herself. Maybe she was about to make a friend she could kid around and laugh with.

They arrived at the Havards' home, a beautiful white stone townhouse four stories tall, graced by iron window boxes brimming with colorful flowers. Mrs. Wescott rang the doorbell, which they could hear chiming inside, accompanied by the barking of a dog.

The door swung open, and a plump woman with a friendly, open face and the frizziest hair Liv had ever seen, beamed as she said, "There you are! Come in, come in!" She stood aside as they entered a large foyer with a stone floor. "Ah, the Wescotts. Lovely!" She pumped Mrs. Wescott's hand. "I'm Tatiana. Delighted to meet you." She turned to Liv. "And this must be our musician—Liv, is it?" Liv nodded and let her hand be engulfed in Mrs. Havard's. The woman's regionless British accent reminded Liv of a television special, where the Queen had greeted guest after guest in refined, well-modulated tones.

As Mrs. Wescott introduced the boys, a small white dog with a very business-like air came forward, sat down in front of Mrs. Wescott, and raised his paw to be shaken.

Mrs. Havard explained, "Baxter's our official greeter. He's a Westie—a West Highland White Terrier. We bought him as a watchdog, but he seems to think he's an ambassador." Baxter wagged his tail furiously and licked each visitor in turn.

"It doesn't matter," she continued. "McGinty's taken over that part of the job." She paused and looked around. "I don't see him any—"

She was interrupted by the sound of beating wings and a blur of green, as a very large macaw swooped down from the top of the staircase, squawking in Liv's ear before it came to land on Anthony's shoulder. "Cool!" he and Cal said together.

The boys might think McGinty was great, but Liv felt she could take him or leave him. While she wondered if he could sense it, the bird flew uninvited from Anthony's shoulder to her head. Mrs. Havard tut-tutted, doing nothing about it at first.

"McGinty has a perch in every room, but he prefers human heads, though he knows better than to try that on us. Visitors, I'm afraid, are fair game."

It didn't seem fair at all to Liv, and she wondered if McGinty had mites. Mrs. Havard frowned at the bird, but he didn't budge—just waited stubbornly for his mistress to come get him. Finally, she picked him up and put him on her own shoulder. Liv wondered if McGinty would think he owed her one now and try to pay her back on her next visit.

No daughter had come out with Mrs. Havard, and Liv felt let down. But as they began to climb the limestone staircase, she heard the sound of a piano. Maybe the girl was practicing. Her new friend.

They wound their way up, and the noise grew louder. Someone was torturing a piano, pounding on the keys with plenty of wrong notes and no attempt to slow down or correct them.

Mrs. Havard never lost her serene expression as she escorted them down a hall that ran the length of the house and bypassed the rooms: a reception room, where the noise was coming from, a large dining room with a giant table piled with stacks of music, and a kitchen, where she stopped and motioned to them. "Here we are. Come right in, everyone."

She pointed to another enormous table and kept walking, detaching McGinty's claws from her sweater and placing him on his perch. He lowered his head and stared at Liv as the family pulled out chairs and seated themselves.

Mrs. Havard's hot, sweet tea was delicious, and the sandwiches, fruit and cookies made Liv realize how hungry she was. Everyone tucked in, and Liv strained to hear her mother and their hostess over the banging of the piano.

Before anyone was ready for second helpings, the battering noises stopped, and the kitchen door swung open. A slender girl with stringy blond hair tramped in. Her watery green eyes, framed by pale lashes, might have been pretty if not for the frown lines between them. "I'm Frederica," she announced, scraping a chair away from the table, and thumping into it. Her mother handed her a plate and pointed to the tray of sandwiches and cakes.

"Well, my dear," she said to Liv, pouring a cup of tea for Frederica and topping off the other cups, "tell me what music you like to play."

Liv politely began listing the pieces she'd be practicing on their piano. "Mozart—I've just begun a sonata. And I'm working on a new Bach Invention." Mrs. Havard's enthusiastic nods and smiles encouraged her to go on. "There's something about the way the melodies twine around each other—"

She stopped when Baxter leaped into her lap and began licking her face. "I hope you like Bach, too, Baxter!" She laughed and hugged him. "You're going to hear a lot of it."

Frederica shot Liv a sour look. "Baxter dislikes counterpoint. He particularly hates Bach." She drank down the last of her tea and brushed crumbs from the white gauze top whose long sleeves were barely paler than her hands. Without a word, she stood and left the room.

"Yeah," whispered Anthony into her ear. "That's because he used to be a Scottie until Princess Pound-a-Lot started playing the piano, and his hair turned white."

Frederica punched out a few more passages with alarming gusto, while the piano and everyone's ears took a beating. Liv felt sorry for Baxter, hunkered under the kitchen table. She could guess why tea had been served here instead of in the dining room— more space between the guests and the noise. Even cheerful Mrs. Havard winced a little now and then. Her shoulders had visibly relaxed when Frederica stopped.

Now the strains of a Chopin Nocturne began to drift through the open transom above the door separating the kitchen from the dining and reception rooms. It was slow, as if she might be just learning it, and her playing was weak. Baxter tolerated it nervously. He settled into an uneasy sleep under the parrot perch, twitching an eyebrow. Liv made a mental note: Ask Mom to pick up doggie treats at Sainsbury's.

As if anxious to steer the subject away from pianos, Mrs. Wescott commented on the stringed instruments they'd seen in the reception room: a small violin in its open case and a half-sized cello on a display stand. Did Frederica play any of those?

"Oh, mercy, no!" Mrs. Havard caught herself. "I mean, not anymore—that is, she used to." She blushed and looked at her husband, who'd wandered into the kitchen to stack a plate with sandwiches.

Mr. Havard, a tall man casually dressed in khaki shorts and a polo shirt, grinned. "Well, come on, one might as well say it—I mean it's no crime to be tone deaf. It's just a crime to deny it." A wrong note on the piano was followed by the bang of a fist on the keys and some rude words. McGinty cocked his head at the sound of Frederica's voice and flew over the door through the transom.

Mrs. Havard said, "We started Frederica out on violin when she was very small, but couldn't stand the out-of-tune problem. We switched her to cello, hoping she'd improve while playing something not quite so high-pitched." Poor Frederica. It didn't sound like much of a cure to Liv, just a way to feel like a failure twice.

Mr. Havard said, "It didn't work, but we let her keep at it for awhile because she seemed to enjoy it. At group recitals, her teacher would slip a cardboard tube from a roll of toilet paper under the bridge of her strings and tell her it was a 'special way for her to play'. She never caught on. When the teacher couldn't take it any longer, we talked Frederica into focusing her talent on the piano."

He sighed as Chopin grew louder and more tortured. "Which, I must say, she plays beautifully on pitch, thanks to our piano tuner." He blinked, refilled his mug with tea, and stood up. "Lovely to meet you, but I'd better retreat to my office and get some work done."

Liv had cringed along with everyone else at the banging. Still, you had to wonder if her parents' complete honesty might be a little hard for Frederica to take.

The afternoon hadn't been a success. The only Havard who wanted to be friends with her was Baxter. McGinty didn't like her much. Mr. and Mrs. Havard were nice enough, but they were grownups.

Then there was Frederica. A total disaster. She was no one Liv would ever pal around with by choice, but it irritated her that she didn't get to make the choice. Who did this girl think she was, disliking her for no reason?

Chapter Twelve

Liv waited with the crowd for the green "Walk" signal. The traffic that screeched to a halt would hurtle down the street again in seconds, and she wanted to be clear of the double-decker bus whose tires nearly grazed the opposite curb. A few stragglers joined her on the narrow pedestrian island, just as the light went red for them. Bus, taxis, cars and a motorcycle—all shot forward at racetrack speed.

Now the traffic came from the left, and after three days in London, the reversal seemed almost normal. Liv focused on not getting run over, but once safely across, she allowed herself the pleasure of observing everything.

Even the broad sidewalk was interesting. Liv was making a mental Things I Like Better about America/Things I Like Better about England list, and the sidewalks had to go down on the England side. A repair crew was smoothing a bed of sand and hoisting new rectangular stones to lay in it. So much prettier than boring concrete, and ready to walk on right away.

Mrs. Havard had called the previous evening to tell Mrs. Wescott that Liv could "pop round" today at ten. So here she was, music books in her backpack, a Mozart sonata streaming through her iPod, taking in the sights and smells of a beautiful June morning in South Kensington. The sidewalks were lined with new-leaved trees, and the azure sky was accented by row after row of tall, white stone buildings. Liv smiled at all of it.

She passed a tiny SmartCar, parked in a pixie-sized space at the curb. Its yellow front and back were paired with black doors, and it looked like an overgrown bumblebee. She could see herself in a red one when she turned sixteen, rather than the MiniCooper that had once been part of her driving fantasy.

Tucked alongside the music in her backpack was the box. Liv, Cal and Anthony agreed that it wasn't safe in their rented apartment, but were at odds over who should be in charge of it. Liv had insisted it was safer with her—the dependable, responsible one. It was a lonely role to play, and neither boy had said goodbye when she left the flat.

She rang the Havards' front doorbell and was immediately buzzed in. The door above swung open, and down the stairs, growling at every step, came Baxter. He took his job as greeter seriously, and harrumphed like a grumpy little watchman who hadn't been expecting to be put on duty so early.

Liv stretched out her hand. "Hey, Baxter, how's it going?" The stubby tail gave two polite wags, and the blunt, wet nose rubbed across Liv's bare toes in her flip-flops. Baxter snorted and turned around to lead the way up the stairs. Two steps up, he halted, turned and leaped back to Liv. The shaggy terrier had to stand on tippaw to sniff the pocket of Liv's capris. Chewsticks! His chin quivered and worked itself up and down as he tried to explain to her how much he loved chewsticks.

"Is that you, Liv, dear? Come on through to the kitchen." Mrs. Havard's cheery voice drifted through the reception room. Liv made her way past the grand pianos with Baxter in the lead. She pushed the door open, entered the kitchen, and scanned the room for attack birds.

McGinty glowed like an evil jewel in the sunbeam that shone on his perch. Liv would have felt better if he'd been in a cage. It took him a full minute to give her a stony stare, one eye at a time.

He chose not to fly over and bite her head.

Mrs. Havard said, "Oh, so you've decided to be friendly today—good boy!"

The macaw lowered his head—a submissive-looking gesture. Liv had never petted a parrot before. She stepped forward and stroked his wing feathers. McGinty leaned into the stroking and closed his eyes as if in rapture.

Encouraged, she reached for the top of his head. McGinty opened his sharp beak wide and cut an eye toward Mrs. Havard, who was occupied filling glasses with orange juice. The beak moved closer, and Liv jumped when Mrs. Havard brought down her palm on the tile countertop with a thwack. "Don't you dare, you beast! I'm sure she's delicious, but she's our guest. That's a fine way to repay her attention, you rogue!"

She spread a piece of toast with Marmite and placed it on a dish with the words, "Spoiled Bird" painted on the side. "Come get your treat, you naughty boy!" It didn't seem like much of a dressing-down for someone who'd just tried to dismember an innocent bystander.

Mrs. Havard pointed to her eyes and back at McGinty, then turned to the stove to deal with a whistling tea kettle. A jump and a wing flap landed McGinty at the end of the counter, where he leaned over as if to pick up his toast. Keeping one bright eye on Mrs. Havard's back, he opened his mouth and stretched toward Liv. Liv broke eye contact and held up her hands, palms forward. McGinty, clearly pleased, took his toast and returned to his perch.

Mr. Havard, in a business suit, burst into the kitchen, grabbed a stainless steel travel mug from the dish rack, and tipped it toward Liv in greeting. "Morning, my dear Liv! Sorry I can't stay and enjoy your playing, but there's only just time to swallow some juice and fill up with Earl Grey." He poured tea into the travel mug, added sugar and milk, and held it out with a straight arm. McGinty swooped over, wrapped his toes around Mr. Havard's wrist and dipped his beak into the steaming liquid. Liv tried not to stare.

Mr. Havard shook the bird off his arm and made his way

toward the hallway. "The Bechstein's my favorite, but we paid more for the Steinway, so there you have it. Take your pick."

He gave Mrs. Havard a quick kiss. "Er, Frederica's. . . in a mood." He picked up a briefcase and was gone. Baxter roused himself to see his master to the front door and Mrs. Havard glanced toward the bedrooms. She sighed, poured another glass of juice, and headed down the hall.

Liv could hear their voices—Mrs. Havard's soothing tones, answered by rapid staccato bursts from Frederica. She returned to the kitchen, gave McGinty a kiss on the beak and Baxter a pat, then pulled a sweater from a wall peg. She took her violin case and shoulder bag from a kitchen chair.

"Well, dear, I'm off to a rehearsal and Frederica's got a French lesson, so we'll leave you and the animals to it. Just lock the door on your way out if we're not back when you finish." She gave a cheerful wave, a striking contrast to the pouty look Frederica shot Liv as she stomped into the kitchen and slammed down her empty juice glass.

Liv resisted the urge to return the look and simply said, "Thanks." McGinty eyed Liv. His owners were barely out the door before Liv was in the reception room with the door closed, Baxter by her side.

She chose the Steinway because it was nearer two enormous windows that looked out over the balcony and the street below. The tops of fresh June trees swayed, tickling the balcony railing.

Liv sat down, reached for the knobs on either side of the bench and began to adjust the height. A cold, wet nose bumped her left hand, and she smiled as she dug in her pocket for a chewstick. She could see he was torn between hating the piano and loving his favorite treat.

Liv shoved the rawhide into his mouth with her left hand and played the entire right hand of her favorite Bach Invention, the one in B Flat Major. He gobbled the treat, relaxing as if he didn't mind the sound.

When she wiped her hand and reached for the keyboard, he whined and traded good behavior for another chewy. This time he was treated to the left hand of the same piece and some ear-scratching.

She had won him over. At least one of the animals in the family disagreed with Frederica's opinion of her.

Liv pulled the book of Mozart Sonatas from her backpack, and Baxter moved as close to her toes as he could without getting hit by the piano pedals. He flopped onto his stomach, stretched out his hind legs, and allowed her to play without further interruption—a clear message to the world that this human, unlike his mistress, knew how to handle people, himself in particular.

She plunged into a difficult passage, playing it slowly, then in different rhythms, until she had mastered it. She became so caught up in the satisfaction of her task and the beauty of the music that she barely noticed Frederica's returning footsteps in the foyer. Baxter snored beside the damper pedal.

"Traitor," Frederica muttered as she passed the opening to the reception room. Baxter opened one eye, then closed it.

Chapter Thirteen

Liv stopped playing and checked her watch—almost twelve o'clock. A few more minutes, and she'd say goodbye to Baxter, lock the door and be on her way. Frederica was nowhere to be seen, but Liv had heard her talking to McGinty. No need to seek her out—she'd just call "Bye" as she left.

She played through a section she'd just memorized, closing her eyes and enjoying the satisfaction of accomplishment. What was it that made her feel someone was watching her? Had it been a slight breeze, or did she hear the faintest creak of a floorboard? Struggling to concentrate, she heard the rich sound of the grand piano vary as if it were bouncing off something near.

Enough—time to go. Reaching for her backpack, Liv felt nothing. With a sinking feeling, she turned around.

The backpack was gone. Her heart dropped all the way to her stomach. She—Liv—the dependable one, had done the unthinkable.

She had let someone take the box.

Panic began to turn to anger, and she walked through the passageway to Frederica's room. The door was open, and

Liv's unzipped backpack lay on the floor. She paused near the threshold and stared, barely suppressing her gag reflex at the sight of Frederica sitting on her bed, sleeves pushed up, methodically making small cuts on her arms with a penknife.

Frederica's face showed no emotion and she appeared not to notice Liv standing there. The cuts she was making now were tiny, but above them were raised scars that looked frightening to Liv. Could Frederica's parents know about this? How could they not?

Liv couldn't imagine what Frederica must experience inside when doing such a thing. She'd heard of cutting before, but it had never occurred to her that she'd know someone who actually did it. It was a frightening thought, and the sight of blood made her queasy.

The girl needed help, but Liv didn't feel like reaching out to someone she barely knew and didn't like. In fact, she could hardly see herself doing it with anyone she did like. In the meantime, she needed that box, and it was on the bed within Frederica's reach.

Frederica looked up, and they locked eyes. Liv lowered hers in revulsion and the absence of anything to say.

Frederica spoke. "I'm sure you hate me. Everyone does. It's part of my life that I accept. The outwardly almost-perfect family—glittering, accomplished parents with a disappointing daughter." The words spilled out in a geyser of bitterness. Liv felt a twinge of pity.

"Now you know my secret. You probably think I'm some sort of horrid freak—a pitiful creature you need to save by tattling to my parents so they can try to get me cured."

Liv had had enough. "Frederica, I'd like to get my property and be on my way. As for saving you, I wouldn't begin to know how, but I can point out that your choice of places to cut is leading you toward a lifetime commitment to long sleeves."

Frederica reached for a bottle of hand sanitizer, squirted the blade of the knife, and pulled a tissue from her jeans pocket. She wiped the blade, over and over. "You're not going to tell my parents?"

Liv opened her mouth to say, "Not if you hand over the box," but shut it. Even though Frederica was annoying, she was actually bleeding. But could she work up sympathy she didn't feel?

Maybe if she pretended to be sympathetic, sympathy would magically grow inside her, as long as she didn't have to hear about cutting. Blood was disgusting. Time to change the subject, distract her, find a chance to grab the box, maybe help Frederica a little along the way.

"Tell me about your dancing." Liv had noticed Frederica's tendency to walk with her toes turned out, the ramrod-straight carriage with shoulders held down, and the bulging calf muscles —she must have had ballet lessons.

Frederica's eyes flickered and she gave a derisive laugh. "That was something I was actually good at—from the time I was very little, and I liked it." She stuck out her legs and flexed her ankles. "By the age of nine, I had broader shoulders than my teacher and bigger feet, and they just kept growing. Try dancing en pointe in size forties, listening to the giggles and whispers."

She hugged herself, the blood from her cuts making small spots on her shirt. "I quit. That was two years ago—the first time I did this. I don't expect you'd understand, but it made me feel better somehow." She examined her arms and reached for a tissue.

Liv looked down at her own size eights and back at Frederica. She guessed the girl's shoe size to be an American nine or ten. It didn't seem like a big deal.

"But quitting dance didn't make you feel better, did it?"

Frederica shrugged and said nothing.

"You could start again, or find something else you love—keep trying. And maybe back away from things you do just to please others, like playing the piano."

Frederica closed the penknife, put it in the back pocket of her jeans, and shook her head. "Oh, I love the piano—it's just myself I hate."

So much for reaching out and trying to help. What were you supposed to say to someone determined to drown in her own problems? She asked, "Why do you do it?"

Frederica picked up the box and whistled for McGinty, who flew in but squawked at the sight and smell of blood. She held out the index finger of her free hand and he reluctantly landed, grasping with his toes and working his way up her arm to her shoulder. He shifted from foot to foot, flapping his wings a little, lowering his head, and working his beak open and closed.

"I don't know why. But sometimes, after a tough day at school or a hurtful remark from Mummy or Daddy, it makes me feel better, like I can see the hurt that's inside instead of just feeling it."

Frederica stroked the top of his head, and the bird closed his eyes and grew still. "But let's change the subject. You know what I think?" She held the box up, shook it like a rattle, and tucked it under an arm. "I think you're not really that interested in my problems. I think you must want this box very much. What's in it—a diary? Letters from a boyfriend? Drugs?"

She stood up and moved toward the open bathroom, still facing Liv. Without a word, she slipped in and closed the door. Liv heard the click of the lock and wondered what to do next. Mrs. Havard might return at any minute and witness the standoff. "Listen, Frederica, I'm really sorry about all the stuff that's bothering you, but that box is mine. I can listen, but please open the door." No reply. It didn't feel right. Frederica liked to complain—the silent treatment wasn't her style. Liv stood perfectly still, straining to listen. Footsteps up the hall and a squawk gave it away.

The bathroom was connected to a room on the other side! Frederica was on her way out. Liv bolted from the bedroom and through the hall as the front door slammed and footsteps thudded down the stairs.

She ran to the window of the reception room and looked out to see which way Frederica had gone: down the steps, toward the Natural History Museum. McGinty was still on her shoulder.

"Sorry, Baxter, you can't come." She jumped over the terrier and closed the door, bounding down the stairs. By the time she reached the stoop, they were out of sight, but unless she disappeared onto a side street, Liv could overtake her.

In only a few minutes, she caught sight of a blond head with a multicolored feathered body beside it. Frederica had started strong, but was slowing down now. Liv decided to drop back, melt into the crowd, and give herself time to think. What would she do with Frederica if she caught up with her? A couple of turns, and they were on Queen's Gate, headed toward Kensington Gardens.

She hung back at the Cromwell Road crossing, putting more people between Frederica and herself, then surged ahead to catch up as they reached the museum. Maybe the exertion of the walk would mellow Frederica.

"I wondered when you'd catch up—took you long enough."

"Where are we going?"

Frederica blinked, as if surprised by Liv's lack of hostility, and looked vulnerable for a moment. Then she shrugged, and the shell was in place again. "I don't know—wherever I feel like going."

It was going to be hard to keep a conversation going. It was like talking to the wind: it still blew the way it wanted, no matter what you said. Liv tried again.

"What's that beautiful round building? Royal Albert Hall? I'd love to see it sometime."

Frederica pursed her lips and exhaled through her aquiline nose. "Mummy's in the Philharmonic, so she's played there. We all know I never will."

They walked awhile more, Liv serving up pleasant comments and Frederica smashing them and seeming to enjoy it. She was tempted to suggest Frederica cut herself some more, but stifled the urge to say it.

They crossed a street and entered Kensington Park, passing the Albert Memorial and Kensington Palace. What little control Liv had over the situation was slipping away. This park joined Hyde Park, and Frederica obviously knew her way around the huge spaces. Liv couldn't afford to lose sight of her or the box.

Finally, Frederica stopped beside the Dutch Garden, a fenced-in area affording a glimpse of beautiful flowers and a pond blooming with water lilies. "I could flatter myself that you're interested enough in me to follow all this way."

She reached up to scratch McGinty with one hand, holding the box with the other. "But, I might as well face it—you just want your ridiculous little trinket. I'm not even sure I care why anymore—it's probably not worth knowing." She eyed Liv up and down and grasped the box with both hands.

Liv held her breath, hoping that Frederica wouldn't do anything foolish, but prepared to spring at her if she did. Frederica seemed to notice the slight change in Liv's stance, and asserted herself by opening the box and shaking it. Drawers lurched open and Liv tackled Frederica, bringing the three of them down on the gravel path.

Chapter Fourteen

"Now look what you've done!" Liv strained to get a better look at the box—she could make out the one and seven notches on the thousands and hundreds drawers. So they were somewhere in the 1700s. The tens drawer was even with its neighbor on the left, the last one barely dislodged.

Seventeen seventy-two, she guessed, glancing down at her flip-flops, then at Frederica's stylishly faded and torn jeans. She'd never time traveled without being dressed properly.

Liv glanced toward the palace and the Orangery behind it. Things didn't appear all that different.

Frederica stood up and began to look around. Liv wondered what she thought of the subtle differences. The lawn was still green, but not clipped to perfection. The Dutch Garden pond was surrounded by a shorter hedge, and the Orangery wasn't crowded with people the way it had been a moment ago. In fact, there was no one in sight—just two out-of-place girls and a parrot.

"We're in the same place, but it isn't the same," said Frederica. "The crowds are gone, the trees aren't as huge, and. . ."

"Exactly."

"Did I do it?"

"Probably." She stepped slowly toward Frederica, reaching out with both hands to take the box. "Just stay very, very still, and I'll try to get us back."

"Back to wh-what?" Frederica stood rigidly still, her eyes open so wide their colorless lashes nearly touched her eyebrows.

"Never mind—I'll explain when we get back."

From the front of the palace came the rumble of male voices, and Liv whispered, "Hide—we need to hide!" The urgency in her voice was contagious, and Frederica crawled along with her in the grass. McGinty dug his claws into Frederica's shoulder.

"Ow!" She pulled at his toes and Liv watched in disbelief as the parrot flapped his wings and soared above their heads. Frederica pursued, leaping and missing him, and dropped the box in the process. Liv longed to make a beeline for it and save herself, but she followed Frederica, and together they watched McGinty land in a chestnut tree branch that overhung the gravel path.

Liv grabbed Frederica's arm and pulled her back. They crouched behind a large boxwood as two men rounded the corner and walked toward them. One wore George Washington-style clothes, cut from silk instead of plain cloth, and as they walked he removed his powdered wig and tucked it under an arm. His uncovered head was completely bald.

His companion, who kept his wig on, was dressed more eccentrically in a long, sleeveless coat of maroon silk embroidered with gold thread, worn over a flowing white shirt. Short red breeches matched the coat, with white hose beneath them.

Three unacceptable things tumbled into Liv's mind at once: the box was out of reach; McGinty was eyeing the head of the bald one; and he looked vaguely familiar.

Her shock turned to fascination when he spoke. "I tell you, Maskelyne—er, Sir Nevil, I'm at wits' end over that rogue Morehouse. All he needs to do is help round up his fellow pirates – there aren't many of them left—and he'd be paid handsomely." He wiped beads of sweat from his head with a silk kerchief. "But he let the word get out that he's bound by some silly sense of loyalty. Imagine! Loyalty to His Majesty is the only kind that counts, and piracy has been out of fashion for years!"

Maskelyne stifled a yawn and made no comment.

"I was counting on a peerage or a baronetcy in exchange for bringing him over to the Crown's way of thinking. Perhaps a title to pass on to my heirs. Lord Cumpston—that has a nice ring to it."

Of course. *Even bald and with no fake tan, there's a resemblance.* The set of the jaw, the hardness of the eyes—they were very much like his modern descendant, Morehouse's partner. And he knew Morehouse!

Liv held her breath and strained to listen. "At the very least, I had hoped for a knighthood or generous land grant if I simply eliminated him."

Maskelyne raised his eyebrows, but Cumpston continued: "But the man is like a shadow. I've pursued him in London, exposed his slight cheating on taxes—no more than most of us, but enough to get him arrested, I thought. I even paid agents to cross the Atlantic and assassinate him in America."

He chuckled. "The fellow did at least leave Morehouse with a good scar to remember him by. Still, the whole business has been most distressing."

They paused under the chestnut branch. McGinty picked off a piece of bark and let it fall from his beak, where it fell close to the men. He unclasped the toes of one foot, stretched, and regripped, pulling himself almost into a split. The other foot followed, until he was positioned perfectly above Cumpston. His eyelids lowered to half-mast and his body went perfectly still.

Liv looked from the bird back to the men. Maskelyne complained: "So you've chased a rogue pirate for a few years? You call that distressing? You can't imagine how I've suffered at the hands of that miserable John Harrison!" He spat out the words. "Having to hear about his precious clocks for decades, traipsing across the world to Barbados on His Majesty's orders to test them, when my way is best—I know it is!"

Cumpston asked, "And how do you know that, Sir Nevil?"

"It relies on the tried and true—the moon and stars—not the latest fantasy of this son of a carpenter, who squanders time in his workshop trying to squeeze a reward from the Crown and all the glory for himself."

Cumpston pursed fleshy lips and clasped his hands behind his back. "And you don't entertain the possibility that he could be right?"

Maskelyne roared, "Well of course not, man, because that would imply I'm wrong!" The multicolored menace crouched, with shoulders hunched and tailfeathers twitching.

Cumpston pulled his hands to the front and studied the lace on his cuffs. "I can see that you really dislike this clockmaker."

"Dislike? Is that what you call it?" The astonomer spluttered, "I detest him, I despise him, I loathe him! He is vermin in my eyes. He is a carbuncle on my backside. He. . .Oh, words fail me to express my disdain for him."

Cumpston continued smoothly, "Yes, yes, I can see how unnerving it might be—someone working tirelessly, inventing things you could only dream of making, capturing His Majesty's attention and finally getting part of the reward he was promised—it all makes you look bad."

Maskelyne made a slight choking sound, which Cumpston ignored.

"I could take care of it for you, ensure that he goes away and never comes back. People will forget about him." He looked at Maskelyne and laughed. "Oh, squeamish, are we? Afraid to take that bold step and—"

Liv gasped as McGinty took perfect aim and dived from his branch straight to Cumpston's head, grabbing pink skin in a three-pronged attack of beak and claws and not letting go.

"Ah-hh!" Cumpston danced around, batting at McGinty and screaming. "Get it off me! Get it off me!" His attacker parried each swat with a vicious peck.

"I'm trying! Can't you see I'm trying?" Maskelyne waved half-heartedly at McGinty, clearly not anxious to dislodge him and become the next victim. He stopped suddenly and turned his head toward the Dutch Garden. "What on Earth?"

McGinty grew tired of the game and flew in the direction of Maskelyne's gaze. Maskelyne ignored the parrot, shaded his eyes with one hand, and squinted. "Who is that? Young boys playing some kind of prank? Trespassing on His Majesty's property?" He ventured no further and turned on his heel to address Cumpston, who was busy blotting drops of blood from his pate with the handkerchief.

McGinty quietly returned to Frederica as if nothing had happened. Liv was taking no chances. She plucked him from Frederica's shoulder and held him close, one hand around his beak. The three remained hidden.

"When you've finished nursing your wounds, go around the back and get the guard dogs' handler. Tell him to turn them loose over there. I must be going—I've an appointment to keep."

Liv held her breath as Maskelyne strode past Cumpston, oblivious to the little brown box lying by a tree trunk, and to the look of contempt in Cumpston's eyes. He banged on a side door of the palace, and a uniformed servant opened it, nodding in deference.

The girls jumped as Cumpston spoke, the sneer on his face creeping into his voice. "Well, Sir Nevil Maskelyne, Astronomer Royal and esteemed scientist, the price of getting rid of your rival has just doubled." He folded his silk square and replaced it in the pocket of his embroidered coat. "Oh, that's right—you didn't ask me to get rid of him—you were horrified at the suggestion. Too bad."

He turned in the direction of Liv's and Frederica's hiding place and narrowed his eyes. "Hmm. . .perhaps I can flush those two out and save myself the trouble of fetching the dog man." He walked along the path, slowly at first, looking all around and stopping every few steps to listen.

Frederica whispered, "We can move over there—in the Dutch Garden. You go get the box. I'll meet you at the end opposite the palace."

Liv looked at the green water in the garden's man-made pond and shuddered. "It's too far—we might not make it, and we'd be trapped with no way out if he saw us. Let's get behind those rosebushes." She pointed to a row full of deep red and golden yellow blooms, tantalizingly close to the box. A ten-yard sprint, and she could get it. If they stayed quiet for a few minutes, maybe Cumpston would give up and go away.

Liv relaxed her hold on McGinty, and he flapped his wings and opened his beak. She sucked in her breath, fearing Cumpston had heard the flaps, and surprised herself by thumping the parrot on the head. He couldn't change his expression, but he cowered. She felt guilty, but hissed, "Shut up, birdbrain—I'm trying to save your life." She crouched lower, hoping the riot of colors in the flowers would make the macaw's brilliance less noticeable. Somehow, McGinty seemed to understand the seriousness of the situation and remained perfectly still.

Frederica was deathly pale, looking like she might throw up or faint. Liv reached for her arm and squeezed it, careful to aim high enough to avoid the new cuts.

Their pursuer walked right past them and disappeared around the corner of the palace. Liv counted to ten and readied herself to spring into action. Then her heart sank as she heard voices.

Here came Cumpston, this time with another man and two huge hounds. Liv couldn't understand what they were saying, but he gestured in their direction and the dog handler nodded. His charges were attached to thin leather leads, stretched even thinner as their quivering bodies lunged again and again. The man strained to keep them from breaking free for now, but Liv didn't have much confidence he would deny them the pleasure of attacking when they found the girls.

From the front of the great house emerged the perfect distraction. A beautifully dressed lady glided down the path, cooing and talking baby talk. *Maybe she'll ask the guy to call off the dogs if she sees them eating us.*

Liv squinted and saw a tiny dog in the lady's arms, its glossy dark coat brushed to perfection and a pink ribbon tied around its neck. The giants had something else to think about for a minute, and they sniffed and jerked their heads around to follow the scent.

That was enough for the lapdog. It yapped ferociously from

the security of its mistress's arms, and the curious brutes bolted, dragging their handler and nearly wrenching his arms out of their sockets. In a blur, the girls took it all in: the shrieks, the shouts, the frantic waving. The lady moved fast for someone with such elaborate long skirts, but she couldn't outrun the hounds. One dog bit the hem of her dress and pulled while the other stood up on his hind legs, paws on her shoulders.

She struggled, and kept both her balance and her dog. But her powdered wig, a work of art nearly a foot tall with sausage curls trailing down her silk-clad shoulders, flew off and onto the path.

Now the dogs had a new prize, better than the yapping thing. They snatched it together and tumbled over each other, pawing and growling. Only when they had ripped it in two were they satisfied, taking off and escaping into the woods beyond the palace, their leashes trailing behind them.

The two men looked at the lady, gazed with longing at the woods where the dogs had escaped, and slunk toward her with bowed heads, their apologies drowned out by her angry screams and the never-ending barking of the furball who had started it all.

"Maybe they're in enough trouble to forget about us for a few minutes," whispered Liv as the unhappy threesome made their way to a door and disappeared inside the palace. "We need to get out of here. You stay—I'll be right back."

She darted across the path, holding McGinty tighter than ever, praying that the hounds wouldn't get tired of the wig and come back for them. Just a few more steps. There—she had it. She crouched and froze as she felt the wind shift.

Trying not to exude the smell of fear, Liv took a few steps and hid behind a tree. Then the inevitable happened. Their scent reached the dogs again, and the baying was furious.

Not caring if they could see her, she ran back to Frederica and knelt to adjust the drawers of the box to take them back to the present. Frederica sucked in her breath. "Listen! They're coming back. Can't you hurry?"

There was no time to reply or do anything except will her

sweaty, trembling fingers to find the correct notches and pull the drawers out. The shouts were coming closer by the second. "Hold on to me!" she screamed, and they were gone.

"Hahh!" Frederica threw back her head and laughed. She stuck out both arms and spun around twice, then landed on the grass and lay there, looking up at the sky and smiling. Liv held McGinty and said nothing.

At last, Frederica sat up and leaned back on her elbows. "I've never felt so alive before—so absolutely exhilarated! We time-traveled, didn't we? I don't care if you glare at me, silent as a statue. I know it's what we did, and it was fantastic! I have thousands of questions, but never mind right now. I just want to do it again!"

Liv felt too angry to speak, but forced herself to look Frederica straight in the eye. "No. It wasn't fantastic."

She tucked the box under her arm and adjusted her grip on McGinty. "And I promise you, you'll never do it again. Try it— tell people about it. I'll make sure you sound like a crazy person. You have no idea what you just did, or how people could have been hurt by it."

She left Frederica sitting in the grass of Kensington Park and began the walk back to the Havards' flat. She had a bird to deliver and a backpack to pick up. The tube ride home to her family's apartment wouldn't be pleasant. Liv would be alone with herself—someone she didn't like very much right now.

Chapter Fifteen

It was Saturday morning, and the Wescott parents and Anna were out for an early morning stroll. At least, the parents would be strolling. Anna was probably riding high in a backpack, pulling on her father's ears and giving the top of his head slobbery kisses.

Liv looked around the quiet sitting room. The boys had been last in the bathroom, and in a minute they'd be ready to talk about what to do today. Liv hadn't yet confessed to them what had happened in Kensington Gardens with Frederica, and she sat in an armchair, working up her nerve.

The bathroom door opened and out came Anthony, followed by a wave of shower humidity. "I need to talk to you two about something," she said.

"Sure, Sis. Cal's on his way." He pulled a banana from a fruit bowl on the dining table and sat on the sitting room sofa that he and Cal pulled open each night for sleeping. It surprised her that he'd said yes so quickly. If she didn't have bigger things to worry about, she'd speculate that something was up and try to pry it out of him.

Cal emerged from the bathroom, looked from Anthony's face to Liv's, and blurted, "I guess Anthony's explaining it to you. We have a problem. Morehouse's partners are serious criminals—killers!" His voice had the high pitch it often took on in times of stress.

Anthony threw up his hands. "Way to go! I thought we agreed to break it to her gently." He rose from the sofa and went to sit on the arm of Liv's chair. He stared meaningfully at Cal, who mouthed *sorry* with a shrug.

Liv gazed out the ten-foot-tall windows at the busy street. "Morehouse could be in real trouble, couldn't he? And I started it."

"It's not your fault, sis. You saw the Cumpston guy, then Cal said a few things to Morehouse, and I said a few things. . ." His voice trailed off.

"Maybe we could just go back," she muttered.

"What? Wait—you haven't heard the rest.

"I Googled the company Morehouse told us about—Cumpston, Pridgeon, and McKnickel. They've been sued a lot, but the plaintiffs always drop the charges before things get very far."

Liv lifted one shoulder. "So? Maybe they offer refunds. Their customers are probably super-rich, hard to please."

Anthony shook his head. "Uh-uh. Here's how the scam works, according to the complaints." He stepped to the mantel, selected a small crystal vase, and held it up for display.

"Say you're a person with something to sell, and you advertise it on the Internet for five hundred dollars. Someone offers to buy it. Great, you say. Their check comes in the mail, but it's for more money than you agreed on, maybe eight hundred." He looked at the vase. "You still have the object, and now you have this guy's check, so no problem, you think. You call him up, tell him about the mistake. He apologizes and asks you to just send the difference along with the item. Maybe he offers to come to you and pick up the cash along with the thing he bought."

He put the vase behind his back, out of sight. "He does all this really fast—before you find out that his check hasn't cleared at the bank. By then, you've sent him the item and some of your money, and he's vanished. Cumpston, Pridgeon and McKnickel have never been convicted of any crimes, but a lot of people think they're guilty."

"It sounds bad," agreed Liv. Her mind wandered back to the problem of Maskelyne and the other Cumpston. She wished she could do some research of her own to see if she needed to be worried about that or not.

Anthony interrupted her thoughts. "It gets worse. These guys buy apartment buildings and say that people on government assistance are living in them. They keep the government checks and rent out the places to other people. They've made a fortune at it."

He rubbed his face with his hand. "It's called housing benefit fraud, and it caught my eye because I've heard Dad say it a couple of times before we came here. I think it's something he's working on, either learning about it so he can help fight it back home or helping someone here. Either way, it could give Morehouse's partners another reason not to like us."

He set the vase back on the mantel, and Cal took over. "It seems Cumpston stays busy now convincing witnesses not to testify against the firm. A few must not've been so easy to convince." He cleared his throat. "They disappeared."

There were voices at the door and the keypad beeped. In came Mr. and Mrs. Wescott with Anna, sound asleep on her father's shoulder. "We wore her out," Mrs. Wescott gasped, collapsing into a chair and leaning back, eyes closed.

"Good thing I don't have to work today," whispered Mr. Wescott. "I'll put her in her crib and lie down on the floor if I can't make it to the bed. Give us a couple of hours and we'll be good as new."

He stopped in the bedroom doorway and turned around. "The Havards called my mobile. They're having a party tonight and we're all invited—even Anna. We won't stay long, but be ready to leave here at seven." He disappeared into the bedroom.

Mrs. Wescott rose from her chair and waved the boys away from the sofa. "Let me have a fifteen-minute power nap and

I'll take you to Madame Tussaud's or the Tower of London—your choice, kids." Before Liv or the boys could reply, she was stretched out, snoring softly.

The scene looked peaceful, normal. Maybe they didn't need to worry about Morehouse or his sleazy colleagues.

And what if she just forgot about the incident with Frederica? No, she couldn't do that, and she couldn't forget about what Frederica was doing to herself.

When she'd had a chance to check historical records and see if anything important had changed because of her trip with Frederica, she'd tell the boys all about it. And maybe she could think of a way to help her. The girl was providing all the bother of having a friend with none of the benefits.

She checked her pocket for her keycard and beckoned to the boys. "Let's go kick the soccer ball around in the alley and give Mom a half hour to sleep. Then I bet she'll take us to Madame Tussaud's and the Tower."

Chapter Sixteen

Liv stayed quiet and kept up her guard. Since the moment they'd arrived at the Havards' party, Frederica had been unnaturally cordial. McGinty treated Liv with newfound respect, bowing his head and avoiding eye contact. Animals were honest. She could mark McGinty off her "enemies" list. But not Frederica—not yet.

Jazz poured from the reception room. Friends of Mrs. Havard had improvised an impromptu concert that blended with the laughter and conversation of the party. Having piled their small plates as high as possible with hors d'oeuvres, Anthony and Cal accepted happily when Frederica invited the three of them to her room.

Only Liv hung back, frowning. Anthony handed her a cup of punch and spoke quietly into her ear. "What's wrong with you, Sis? There's plenty of food, the bird's behaving itself and Frederica can't get near a piano to torture us with her playing. Enjoy it!" Liv sighed and followed the boys down the hall.

Frederica stood by her dresser, a smug expression blanketing her face. It was the look of someone who had the upper hand.

"What do you want?" Liv asked bluntly.

"You know perfectly well," she replied. "I told you I want to do it again, and I meant it." She looked at the boys, who had stopped chewing to stare at her.

"Why?" asked Liv.

"Because it's fun, in spite of what you say." She rolled her eyes at Liv. "And I'm curious—who wouldn't be?" She kicked off her shoes and sat down on her bed, legs crisscrossed. "It's the ultimate escape—like jumping live into the middle of a fantastic computer game. It's someone else's reality."

Cal and Anthony exchanged stunned looks. "It's obvious you've time-traveled somehow," began Anthony, "and we didn't know about it. But—"

"You don't know how it works," interrupted Liv, avoiding Anthony's glare. "What's to keep us from leaving you?"

Frederica smirked. "Oh, let me count the ways. . .First, you'd never do that—you're all such rule-followers." She turned to Anthony. "Second, it's that same 'we have to be so-o-o responsible' mindset that's going to make you go back and correct the little problem your sister and I accidentally caused the other day."

She watched the boys' faces and her smile broadened. "Oh, she didn't tell you? We got somebody killed."

"What?" Anthony jumped to his feet and ran to his sister's side. "What's she talking about?" Cal sat frozen upright in his place at the window seat.

"I don't know," said Liv miserably. "This part is new."

Frederica continued, "We didn't really change anything important. You'd never have known if I hadn't told you. I'd never have known if I hadn't happened to go on a school field trip to Greenwich Observatory last year."

She raised a shoulder and lowered it in a dismissive gesture. "John Harrison, inventor of the watch that solved the problem of finding longitude at sea, died a disappointed old man in seventeen seventy-six. I remembered that from the field trip."

Liv's voice was barely a whisper. "And now he died in seventeen seventy-two, because of us?"

"Exactly. He got himself poisoned by one of the men who

saw us in Kensington Gardens, a fellow named Cumpston."

Liv watched as Cal's mouth popped open at the mention of Cumpston's name. Anthony crossed his arms and frowned, but Frederica continued her story, and Liv hoped desperately she wouldn't drop Morehouse's name. The boys would never understand why she'd keep that from them.

"My guess is that Maskelyne, the Astronomer Royal, was about to tell Cumpston he wasn't all that angry at Harrison, but we interrupted and he missed his chance." She paused and pointed to the computer on her desk. "I checked it out thoroughly this morning. Cumpston poisoned him, all right." Cal blew a puff of air from his cheeks, and Liv lowered her head and closed her eyes.

Frederica pursed her lips. "Harrison's long dead and gone anyway. I don't see why you feel the need to make a fuss. An old man died a few years early—no big deal.

"Now, don't you want to hear about the third reason you'll want to take me with you when you go back to fix the problem? Such a simple thing: you don't have the clothes. Mummy and her friends play string quartet gigs at castles and places all over. I can get my hands on just about anything you need, which means you need me."

No one contradicted her. Period costumes could be rented, but that would cost money and require an explanation to Mr. and Mrs. Wescott. Frederica had them right where she wanted them.

Anthony took a bite of smoked salmon and made a face. Eyeing a bag of Walker's crisps on the dresser, he rose and crossed the room. He pulled out a crisp and placed a piece of salmon on it, devouring it in one bite. "Who was actually holding the box when the three of you traveled?"

Frederica looked from one to another. "Why is that important?" she demanded. "I was holding it. McGinty was on my shoulder. Liv tackled me, and off we went." She squinted at Anthony. "What does it mean?"

"It doesn't mean anything!" Liv grabbed Anthony's arm and dug in. "You don't know if she controlled it, and we're not sending her back alone." Liv knew that the box worked only for certain people, but she wasn't about to allow for the possibility that Frederica could be one of them.

"Of course not, Sis, but someone needs to go and undo this mess. Having her along might not be a bad idea."

"Not a bad idea? She went once, and look what happened!"

Cal interrupted, "Has everyone lost their minds but me? We have a life-and-death situation, and you want to bring in a wild card?" He nodded at Frederica.

Anthony held up his palms. "She knows more about London than we do—knows how to get to Greenwich Observatory to find this astronomer at home, I hope. When she speaks, she doesn't have an American accent."

He pulled up a stool and sat directly in front of Frederica. "You haven't done anything to make us willing to trust you, but you owe it to this man Harrison and his family to try to save him."

His voice softened. "And one thing we've learned from our own mistakes: What people do ripples out and affects others a long way into the future. Cumpston's descendants won't be better off for what you let him get away with. Agree to go for the right reasons and we'll let you do it."

Frederica's shell seemed to open just a little. "Agreed."

Chapter Seventeen

Monday morning came with a gray sky that cast its shadow on the city below. Even the summer flowers, abundant on buildings everywhere, appeared solemn in the hazy light.

To Liv, it made sense that Maskelyne, not realizing what Cumpston was planning, would have returned to his apartments and his work at the Observatory in Greenwich.

If they were lucky, a single trip there to warn the Astronomer Royal of what was coming would be enough, and Maskelyne could take it from there. What if he didn't believe them? Liv decided not to consider that possibility. They'd just have to be convincing.

Frederica had agreed to meet her in Kensington Park. Their parents had been surprised at the sudden blossoming of a friendship between the two girls, but happy enough about it to give them permission to spend the day around London. Only Cal and Anthony knew the truth.

She strolled up the gravel path, past the Dutch Garden, and took a seat on one of the park benches that dotted the double rows of giant boxwoods leading to the Orangery. The smell of fresh-cut grass was sweet.

Her only company was a woman seated on the next bench, dressed in jeans and a light jacket, covered with pigeons. They perched on her head, bickered for favorite spots on her shoulders, arms and legs, and nibbled at breadcrumbs in her outstretched hands. Liv gave up trying not to seem rude and gaped openly. The pigeons must respect the woman—none of them had pooped on her, yet.

"You'd better practice being more alert—I completely sneaked up on you." Frederica, wearing a flowing white blouse with her jeans and carrying long skirts and another blouse over her arm, slid onto the bench next to Liv. Her characteristic sneer was gone. If Liv hadn't known better, she could have passed for human.

"Take this blouse. You can pull it over your tank top, right here before we leave. Put the skirts in your backpack and carry them for us. Mummy has no idea I've taken her things, so we need to be careful with them. You're welcome, and I hope you remembered to bring your little box and your travel pass."

Liv tried biting her tongue to keep herself from snapping back at Frederica. It worked. It hurt so much, she couldn't even remember what she'd wanted to say. There was a pause as she checked her mouth for the taste of blood.

"Well, don't you think we'd better get on with it?" asked Frederica, folding the skirts and looking down at the blouse.

"Sure."

The girls walked along the sidewalks to the High Street Kensington tube station. Frederica seemed to drop her guard, and they enjoyed window-shopping, with Frederica pointing out the most fashionable shops.

"Why don't you tell me how we're getting to Greenwich?" Liv asked.

"Well, we have a choice. Take the Jubilee Line to North Greenwich, or get ourselves to Charing Cross Station to catch a train. Or we can go my favorite way."

"None of it means anything to me. So what's your favorite?"

Frederica almost smiled. "It's taking the Docklands Light Railway. We can catch it at Tower Hill. I love getting out from under the ground, seeing where I'm going."

"Sounds good." Liv almost smiled back.

They stepped off the train at Greenwich, Frederica taking the lead. There had been several empty cars on the driverless train, and choosing one had given them the chance to pull their long skirts on over their jeans.

They made their way out of the station and onto the streets, which were becoming crowded with tourists. A few minutes of walking brought them to an intersection.

They paused in front of a shop, where a bowed window displayed a huge pie on a stand. The golden, flaky crust glistened in the sunlight that streamed through wavy old glass. The shop's open door had invited a few flies, who performed an aerial insect ballet around the pie. Liv couldn't blame them.

Frederica stopped with Liv and followed her gaze. "Didn't know you fancied eel."

"What? No, it can't be. Tell me that's something delicious, like apple or cherry."

"Afraid not. But I like the age of the place. There's a chance it may have been here for a very long time, and it looks like a good spot for us to use your box."

"Are you sure we're close enough to the Observatory? I don't want to walk through the whole town in seventeen-seventy-two."

Frederica laughed. "Stop worrying, will you? This is an adventure, and we're doing a good deed at the same time."

Liv could have argued the point that undoing a bad deed wasn't quite the same as doing a good one, but she reached into her backpack for the box without protest. Then she pulled out the drawers while Frederica clutched her arm.

She knew they had traveled before they opened their eyes— she could smell it. She freed herself from Frederica's grip and gaped at the stall across the street, where a Starbucks had been a moment ago.

Vendors were processing and selling fish in the space. A stout woman with raw, chapped hands and rolled-up, grimy sleeves was hacking off fish heads and dropping them into a rough wooden bucket. With a final thwack she beheaded her last victim, tossed the head into the bucket and slung the body onto a stained plank, fresh and ready for sale.

A graying, toothless man beside her grinned and reached deep into a barrel, drawing out a huge gray eel for a customer. The buyer nodded as the man hoisted the slimy, limp form with one hand and gestured broadly with the other.

The customer frowned and kept his eye on the scale, ignoring the fishmonger's attempt at distraction and pointing at the weight. A few seconds of haggling over the price and the satisfied buyer walked away, his dinner in a string bag dripping spots of brine water onto the cobblestones.

"Give me a minute to get my bearings," whispered Frederica. "It's all a bit much to take in at once."

Liv knew the feeling. "Take your time."

Leaving Frederica to process her emotions, Liv turned and looked behind them, wondering if the shop with the eel pie would be there. Sure enough, the same modest brick building rose from a cobbled sidewalk, the sagging of age gone.

The glazing for the windows was in place, but it did nothing to keep flies from floating in the front door on the intoxicating aroma of baked eel flesh and lard pastry. On a glass stand in front of the middle window stood a ringer for the eel pie the girls had seen moments before in their own century.

As they threaded their way through the crowd and away from the market, Liv continued inhaling through her mouth, exhaling through her nose. It didn't help. She could taste it that way: brackish water, raw fish, moldering vegetables and open pails of raw milk—one big nauseating mix with an undertone of horses and unwashed bodies.

She followed Frederica across the cobblestone square and onto a broad road, determined not to throw up or fall behind. The raw fish odor retreated, but there were horses everywhere, and a warm manure stench advanced to take its place. Liv marveled at Frederica, who didn't seem to be the least bit affected.

"How can you stand it?"

Frederica turned and looked around. "Stand what?"

"The smell."

She followed Liv's gaze to a horse relieving itself in the middle of the street and shrugged. "Sinus problems."

They were still blocks away from the Observatory and the hill leading up to it.

Liv suspected that Frederica was taking a scenic route. A few turns should have taken them to King William Walk and right to Greenwich Park, but they'd passed the Royal College and the graceful Queen's House and seemed now to be backtracking.

She didn't feel like fighting over the issue, so she just said, "If I sweat all over your mom's blouse, it'll be your fault, you know."

Frederica seemed to get the point. "Oh, right. Sorry about the detour. I just couldn't resist. And it is beautiful without all the asphalt and cars and noise, isn't it?"

"It is," agreed Liv.

They turned, almost companionably, into the park and began the long climb to the Observatory grounds.

Chapter Eighteen

"Now what do we do?" Liv spoke the words more to herself than to Frederica.

The courtyard of Flamsteed House, their destination and the home of Sir Nevil Maskelyne, was deserted.

"Simple," answered Frederica. "Pick a door and knock on it."

"I can figure out that much," grumbled Liv. "This one has handrails at the steps. Maybe it's more important." She walked toward the door, trying to think of what to say. As they reached the first step, a brass doorknob, set squarely in the middle of the door, turned.

The door opened and a middle-aged lady in what might have been a Betsy Ross costume gave a cry of surprise. She frowned at them. "See now, it won't do you any good to come asking for work around here. We don't need a lot of staff—Sir Nevil lives alone, and he doesn't entertain much."

Before Liv could reply, the woman's expression softened, and she continued, "If you're hungry, just slip in and go down to the kitchen. Cook'll give you a bite to eat."

"Thank you!"

"Oh, it's no trouble. Now go on, before anyone sees me acting soft!" She stood aside and pointed the way down a flight of stairs.

They walked as directed until they were out of the woman's sight, then Frederica whispered, "We need to get back upstairs and start looking for Maskelyne. We'll try the Transit Room and the Zenith Sector first, then go on from there if we have to."

"Whatever you say. I have no idea what you're talking about."

"I took the tour—remember?" Frederica opened a door, and the girls tiptoed into a large room with a wooden floor and whitewashed walls. The exposed rafters were whitewashed as well, and with sunshine pouring in the large windows, the effect was cheery. A handful of large, mysterious instruments that Liv assumed were for viewing or calculating dominated the space, but no one was there.

"Next stop, Zenith Sector." Frederica said.

"What's that?"

"It's a really long telescope," she explained. "I can't think how anyone would use it during daylight, but Maskelyne's probably somewhere in the building, making rounds, checking equipment, which means we need to make the rounds ourselves."

This time they were rewarded. The astronomer sat in an armless reclining chair, polishing the lens of what looked to Liv like a giant periscope. Notebooks lay scattered on the floor, along with a quill pen and inkpot. He was totally absorbed in his task.

"Ahem." Liv cleared her throat, hoping not to startle him. Maskelyne sat up suddenly and hit his head on a wooden cross-piece bracing the telescope.

"Mrs. Perkins!" he shouted, holding his head with both hands and keeping his eyes shut. "Have I not made it perfectly clear that I am not to be disturbed when I am in this position? I have banged my head on this insufferable thing more times than I care to count, and—Oh. . ."

His eyes open only to a squint, he peered at the girls without recognition. Then, stabbing the air with a finger, he said, "You!

You look familiar. Where have I seen you?"

"Kensington Palace, Sir Nevil, in the gardens," answered Liv.

"I don't remember any young girls at Kensington."

Frederica explained, "You may have thought we were dressed like boys. We had a macaw—your people had dogs. Remember?"

Maskelyne scrambled from his seat, lunged forward, and grabbed Frederica by the arm, narrowly missing the inkpot with his foot. "Of course! Out with the both of you—I should have you arrested. Shoo! Shoo!" He let go of her and made fanning motions at them with both hands. They stood still.

"Away! You're not gone—I ordered you out! How is it that you're still here?"

Liv said, "Sir Nevil, we have to talk to you. We've come a very long way to see you—you have no idea how far."

She looked over her shoulder to be sure that Maskelyne's shouting hadn't brought any servants running to his aid. "It's about those things you said to Mr. Cumpston—sounding like you wanted him to get rid of your rival."

The astronomer paled, recovering as he protested, "That was a private conversation, and if you intend to make any groundless accusations, remember that the word of two underage, trespassing eavesdroppers won't be worth a half-penny.

"Now, I'm leaving the room and returning to my apartments. I suggest you find the way out before I have to call someone to help you find it."

He turned on his heel and walked out. Liv and Frederica looked at each other, shrugged, and followed him.

They caught up with him as he stopped at a paneled door, taking a large key out of his pocket and inserting it in the lock. Liv tried clearing her throat one more time.

"Aaaah!" He whirled around and held his hand over his heart. "Must you continue to surprise me in this fashion?" He turned the key and opened the door, motioning them in. "Since you insist, I'll give you a moment of my time." He followed them into a sitting room, leaving the door open. "State your business, then off you go."

"Just like we said, it's about that Cumpston man and what he said he'd do to your enemy," Liv began.

"Stop! Stop!" he demanded. "I heard him speak of nothing specific. And if by enemy, you mean John Harrison, my official position is that I hold him in the highest regard. No one can accuse me of any feelings of prejudice against him."

At the mention of Harrison's name, a squawk emanated from the next room. "Harrison! Blast Harrison! My life's work! My life's work!"

Frederica sucked in her breath. "You have a parrot in there! May we see it?"

Maskelyne nodded and stared at the floor. "Bah! I shouldn't have spoken Harrison's wretched name. I didn't mean to get her started."

He closed his eyes and rubbed his forehead. "It's just Precious. There's no use pretending. She's only repeating what she's heard me say a thousand times."

He walked toward an open door, and motioned for them to follow. "Come, I'll show you."

Chapter Nineteen

They entered a low-ceilinged room, furnished simply but elegantly. The narrow four-poster bed was tucked into an eave, with brocade curtains of heavy red silk reaching from ceiling to floor. An ornate chest of dark wood stood at the foot of the bed, with a large china chamber pot placed conveniently nearby.

A round table, covered with more red silk, fringed at the bottom, held a cup and water pitcher, candlestick and a long wig on a stand. A huge gilt frame mirror and gold wall sconce complemented the oriental rug on the parquet floor. A red velvet robe and house slippers were set out.

Liv wondered if she should feel uncomfortable at being invited into such a private space, but Maskelyne paid no attention to the girls. He walked straight to a brass cage, where a macaw as large as McGinty hopped up and down at the sight of her master. She was almost completely ruby red, with accents of blue, green and gold on her wings and tail.

"You'll probably fancy her. Would you like to have her? You could take her as a companion for that outrageous specimen you had with you the other day."

He reached for the latch and Precious waited politely, shifting her weight from foot to foot. Maskelyne offered his arm, and she flew out, bypassing him and making straight for Frederica's shoulder.

Instead of becoming irritated at his lack of control, he simply rolled his eyes and smiled. "Well, that's typical of Precious. Swans about like she owns the place."

He laughed. "I remember when I bought her in Barbados. I was there on His Majesty's orders, testing Harrison's timepiece, and while I was at it, would I please pick up a parrot for Her Majesty the Queen? That made a dismal trip even worse." He shuddered at the memory and the smile disappeared.

"There were birds for sale at a roadside market, behind a dusty old canvas in a filthy wooden cage. I nearly bought one for myself, thinking it would be like having a brightly-colored chicken—nothing that would live on year after year, demanding attention and special food and getting continually into mischief."

Precious left Frederica's shoulder and hopped onto the bedside table, stealing a bite of hair from his wig and flying from the room. He followed her and the girls trailed along, entering the great Octagon Room. Precious flew up, up, up, where she perched on the plasterwork frieze above a portrait of King Charles I, nearly twenty feet above their heads.

He continued, "I didn't buy a bird that day, but later, in a pub, I saw this gorgeous fowl." He pointed at Precious, who cocked her head at him and yelled, "Buy me a drink! Buy me a drink!"

Maskelyne grinned sheepishly. "Perhaps it was the bottle of rum the barkeep poured from so freely, but at the end of the night, I was the proud owner of Precious and poorer by several gold pieces. The king was happy enough to ask me to bring a bird home to him, but never offered to pay for it."

Precious dived from the frieze but slowed as she neared them, landing delicately on Frederica's shoulder again, this time rubbing her head against the girl's hair. "I think she smells McGinty," said Frederica, rubbing the bird's beak with her finger.

Precious closed her eyes and swayed contentedly. "Closing time! Closing time!" she called.

"Isn't her repertoire a little inappropriate for the Queen?" asked Liv.

Maskelyne shook his bald head. "I never had the chance to worry about it. By the time I returned from Barbados, Queen Charlotte had acquired a cockatoo. I couldn't get rid of Precious because His Majesty insisted I keep her, just in case the Queen might ever want her." He folded his arms. "She didn't, of course, and this is the third wig, among other things, that she has delighted in chewing on."

"Well, I can solve that for you," Frederica offered. "She likes the powder—not the wig. All parrots like to eat clay in the wild—it neutralizes the toxins in the foods they eat. Our macaw used to get into my mother's face-mask powder all the time, because it's kaolin-based." Maskelyne looked appreciative, and Liv was intrigued. The girl could be helpful when she wanted to.

"We used to scold him for it," she continued, "and he'd squawk, 'Not me! Not me!', but the dusty beak was a giveaway. Now that we know he needs it, we furnish him with a bit of clay to eat now and then."

"Thank you," said the astronomer. He looked at the girls and waited.

Liv held up a hand and said earnestly, "Don't ask us how we know, just trust us when we tell you that Cumpston is up to no good. We don't know the details, but he's going to kill Mr. Harrison with poison—soon. You have to stop him!"

"I have to stop him?" he replied petulantly. "And just how do you propose I do that?" He turned and spoke to the air, "Oh, Cumpston, that murder which I did not request you do—you know the one? Well, don't do it, because those ridiculous girls reappeared to me—without their parrot this time—and said you shouldn't." He crossed his arms and stared at them.

Liv's mind raced through a dozen possibilities. Maskelyne didn't seem to want Harrison dead—he just didn't believe them. Maybe they could find some evidence and come back tomorrow, try again to convince him. Maybe they could find John Harrison and warn him. Maybe, maybe.

While she racked her brain for alternatives, Maskelyne

seemed to have a change of heart. "Perhaps you're right about talking to Cumpston," he said, "although you couldn't possibly know the future."

Liv's stomach lurched, and she stole a glance at Frederica.

Maskelyne took no notice and rattled on, "It's not an easy thing to put him off, and you don't want to be on his bad side. It's common knowledge that he does things."

"Things," repeated Frederica. "Like. . ."

Liv finished the thought. "Like making your enemies disappear."

Maskelyne shook his head. "I don't think he's as extreme as all that. Here's a more benign example: Say you have a tea shop, and it's not doing well. You're losing customers to the shop down the street. Cumpston can arrange for a shipment of your competitor's tea to arrive late. Rumors will spread that he cheats customers by mixing dried grass into the tea. The glass in his front window may be smashed overnight.

"Or say your neighbor's dog is killing your chickens. The dog might simply disappear. Or, for a higher fee, one of the neighbor's chickens might appear on his doorstep, slaughtered and torn to bits."

He continued, "Cumpston knows how to get things done, and if he were more stable, he'd actually be useful."

He reached out to Precious and stroked her wing feathers. "I am comfortable with believing that society has a place for people like him, but he's unreliable. He loves power and becomes obsessed easily, as he is with that pirate he's been chasing for years.

"Ironic, isn't it? I've been obsessed with beating out John Harrison all these years, and look how it caused this present difficulty with Cumpston. Harrison harbors no good feelings for me, either, though I suppose I've earned some of that."

He faced them. "The Longitude Board ordered me to confiscate all four copies of H4, and I did it with great enthusiasm. It did not endear me to the man, I must say."

Frederica interrupted, "We'll take care of telling Cumpston to stop." Her eyes were no longer haughty, but kind. "Just tell us where we can find him. If he knows we're on to him, he may back off, and if he tries anything, we know how to disappear in a hurry."

Maskelyne nodded.

Liv added, "We'll warn Harrison, too."

"No!" Maskelyne undid the top frog of his high-collared vest and loosened his white silk neck scarf. "I've hated him for years. I'll admit I've nursed a grudge that's grown to be an old friend." He removed his wig and mopped his bald head, which had turned crimson along with his face. "But kill Harrison? Never."

He pointed to a pitcher on a carpet-covered table and gave Frederica a meaningful look. She took the hint and poured water into a mug for him, which he took without thanks, sinking heavily into a velvet-upholstered chair.

The Astronomer Royal's color quickly returned, and he continued as if nothing had happened. "Though I loathe the notion of giving Harrison aid, I shall take it upon myself to warn him. He won't have the decency to thank me, I'm sure, but I don't wish the old curmudgeon to come to an untimely end.

"Now, if the two of you are willing to confront Cumpston and convince him to lay aside his sorry plot, you could do it tomorrow evening. I'm hosting a reception here in the Great Star Room for members of the Board of Longitude.

"Since I've taken pains to convince them not to trust Harrison and his infernal timepieces, I thought it would be the perfect opportunity to invite the King and Queen—" He smiled at the girls' widened eyes "—and sway them completely over to my way of thinking. His Majesty still leans a bit too far in Harrison's favor for my peace of mind."

He sighed. "Saving his sorry hide may cause me to forfeit that opportunity." He stroked the powdered wig in his hands and fell silent.

Liv wondered if he would decide not to help them after all, but he surprised her. "It will be a small matter to invite Harrison at short notice, and Cumpston will fall over himself with delight if I invite him as well. We could kill two birds with one stone." He caught himself and frowned. "Hmm. . .unfortunate choice of words. Now, if you plan to attend my small soiree, please do not come dressed in those very odd costumes."

Frederica drew in a breath. Liv placed a hand on her arm, but not soon enough to stop her from bristling at the criticism. "What's wrong with them?"

The astronomer pressed his thin lips together and exhaled a snort. "They're too fine for peasant or scullery maid garments, not fashionable enough for a well-paid house servant, certainly not suitable for a gathering of gentle or royal people."

Frederica whispered to Liv, "They're musicians' costumes, designed to blend into the background for all occasions, so they're not perfect for any one time period."

Liv was out of her depth. Maskelyne mistook their lack of answer for an invitation to explain more. "What do I know of women's clothes?" he spluttered. "The sleeves are too long, there's too little trim, the cut of the neckline and shoulders is peculiar. They simply don't look right." He eyed them again and said, "It's as if you poured the fashions from several decades into a pot and stirred them together into one distasteful stew." His words made Liv's stomach drop.

Relax, she told herself. If there's a little of the future in these clothes, he won't know the difference. It's just a small mistake. But even small mistakes could cause big trouble. That much she knew.

She forced herself to smile. "Thank you, Sir Nevil. We can meet you about this time of day tomorrow. And there may be four of us, with my brother and his friend."

Maskelyne began retying his white silk neck scarf. "I'm sure that won't do, it won't do at all. I have a reputation— quite undeserved, of course—for being difficult to get on with, especially with children."

"Children?" Frederica leaned forward into the astronomer's face, challenging him to say another word.

He ignored her and continued, "It would strain the imaginations of everyone who knows me that I would tolerate even a single visitor, but four guests? Impossible!"

Liv brushed a tiny red feather from her velveteen skirt and

narrowed her eyes at Maskelyne. "Excuse me for being frank, Sir Nevil, but you're in for a world of trouble if we don't get this Cumpston fellow to change his plans. And if he's caught for poisoning Mr. Harrison, do you think he'll take all the blame for it?"

Liv felt a twinge of guilt as Maskelyne began to fan himself again, but she pressed on and asked Frederica, "What's the penalty for being an accessory to murder? Do they still use the Tower of London to hold prisoners?"

"Stop! Stop!" he begged. "Of course you may bring guests. My life will be in shambles if we don't get this thing stopped. I can introduce you as my nieces."

He held up his arm and beckoned to Precious, who turned her head away from him and refused to leave Frederica's shoulder. The old astronomer threw up his hands and turned to leave the room. "I have many things to attend to, and I'm sure you young ladies do as well. As soon as you can extract that bit of feathered pestilence from yourselves you may find your own way out."

He left the room and called from the hallway, "Or take her with you. It's of no consequence to me."

Chapter Twenty

Liv slipped behind Frederica. "I'll just grab her like I did McGinty. You get ready to slam the cage door shut."

Precious dug her claws into Frederica and screamed, "Back in the cage! Back in the cage! No!"

"Ow!" Frederica pulled at the claws and got her hand pecked for it. "Ow, again!"

She frowned at Liv. "Stop helping—will you? She's killing me!" She tried coaxing Precious, inching a finger toward her again. "Come on, pretty bird, just step onto it." The macaw refused to budge.

"I think we can trick her," offered Liv. "Ignore her. Keep talking to me and walk slowly toward the c-a-g-e." Precious gave another scream and lowered her head. "Uh-oh, she knows what that spells."

A tear trickled down Frederica's cheek, though her expression never changed. The macaw's grip must be ferocious. "I've changed my mind about your helping. Here's what we can do: Stand in front of me. I'll turn suddenly, you use both hands to secure body and beak, and I'll take care of the claws. Ready, set, go!"

With a quick attack and a little luck, they captured her and stuffed her into her cage before she could react. Frederica shut the door, but had to forgo locking it in favor of moving her fingers out of harm's way as the indignant parrot snapped at them.

"How can anybody stand her?" Liv asked as she pulled the box out of a deep pocket of her skirt and opened the latch.

Frederica inserted a thumb at the side of the wide neckline of her blouse and inspected her shoulder. "I think she's not so bad— just a bit desperate for attention."

"If you say so. Hang on to me. Here we go."

Frederica took Liv's arm, Liv pulled at the drawers of the box, and Precious threw the unlocked cage door open and propelled herself like a shell from a howitzer, landing right back on Frederica's shoulder before the three of them disappeared from seventeen seventy-two.

"I know a source for the perfect clothes." Frederica led the way down the steeply descending walkway from Flamsteed House, ignoring the passersby who pointed and stared at Precious. They'd been fortunate enough to find themselves alone in the astronomer's apartment when they'd returned to the present, but getting outside with Precious had seemed problematic. In the end, the simplest solution worked. They walked straight out, slipping into an empty room once to avoid a tour guide.

Now that she could ride Frederica's shoulder unchallenged, Precious was completely docile, making little cooing and gurgling noises and rubbing Frederica's head with her own.

Frederica continued, "That is, the source is perfect except for one thing. We'll have to pretend to be the best of friends, getting along famously and eager to have a girly evening together, playing dress-up." She led the way off the path and into the grass, stopping beside an empty park bench. She slipped off her long skirt, revealing jeans underneath. Liv did the same and folded both skirts around the box, carrying it all in a bundle.

They returned to the path and continued their descent. Frederica said, "Mummy has a friend who's wickedly rich and loves to put on costume balls for charity functions. We can ask her to borrow two dresses, I think."

Liv frowned. "Pretend to be friends."

"That's it."

"Give the lady a call."

Chapter Twenty-one

Delighted that her daughter appeared to be getting along well with anyone, Mrs. Havard wasted no time making the phone call to her costume-owning friend, and the girls had an invitation to the home of Mrs. Philomena Davison for the next day.

Mrs. Havard gave them cab fare for the ride home, since they would be carrying their costumes, but they took the tube to Mrs. Davison's house.

"Your mother must be the nicest person ever," Liv said as they left the platform area and stepped onto a steep escalator that would carry them from the bowels of the earth up to street level. "Calling Mrs. Davison, paying for the cab, and putting up with Precious. I think you'll end up keeping her, by the way—we both know no one's going to answer your mom's Found Bird ad. And McGinty would never survive the heartbreak if she left."

It was true. The girls had brought the macaw back to the Havards' flat, not quite sure what to do with her, and McGinty had been smitten from the moment he'd set his beady eyes on her. He'd stared, beak open, for a full five minutes, as if he couldn't believe she wasn't a dream.

Precious, out of sorts from having been smuggled all the way from Greenwich, wrapped up in Liv's shawl and carried by Frederica, had given an impatient squawk that sent McGinty scurrying to find food, toys, and trinkets to bring to this vision of loveliness. By the next day they were inseparable, a pair of real lovebirds.

Frederica led the way out of the tube station and down the street, turning left after two blocks, then again and again, looking up at the street signs secured at second-story height to the buildings. As they made their way along, drab buildings with shabby little shops on the ground floors gave way to nicer ones with expensive-looking boutiques.

A few more turns, and the girls were walking down a quiet street where stately houses boasted small front yards, meticulously landscaped.

"This is it," Frederica said, turning up a brick walk leading to a house swathed in a flamboyant mix of climbing roses in every color. Of course the owner liked costumes, Liv thought. She'd even dressed up her house.

They rang the bell, and the door opened at once. A plump lady with warm hazel eyes and hair tinted a vague shade that was neither blond nor brown stood before them. "Well, come on then, dears, you must be Frederica and her friend. Now, which is which?"

She held up her hand for silence while she looked them over carefully. "Got it!" she declared, beaming at Frederica. "Your mother's eyes and creamy complexion, your father's jaw and slender build." She paused. "Not sure where the blond hair came from. But you're definitely Frederica."

Liv liked her immediately. "That's very good," she said, as Frederica blushed and remained silent.

Mrs. Davison led the way through a spacious foyer and up a curved staircase. "I'm a widow," she said, as if someone had asked her a question. "I married a man who made a lot of money with his business, but it seemed no one wanted to let me forget that I was from humble roots, so I never did. Instead of brooding about it, I've had great fun inviting girls from the poorest neighborhoods over for teas and dinners and dress-up parties, especially since my Harold died."

She stopped on the landing, a huge space tiled with black and white marble squares, and inspected two giant banana plants in lead tubs, sticking her forefinger into the dirt of each one and nodding.

"And of course there are the charity balls. We've raised money for several worthy causes." She pointed to Frederica and said, "You should come help me, dear. Get you out from under your Mum's and Dad's shadow."

She turned again and continued up the staircase, missing Frederica's frown. She led them down the main upstairs hallway, past door after door, all closed, all carved identically and painted white. Liv wondered how she remembered what led where.

"Now, I have lots and lots of dresses, but I think I know the perfect ones for you two," she said, stopping at a door and turning its brass knob. She looked at Liv. "Tatiana told me you two are interested in the late seventeen hundreds, especially the seventeen-seventies. Is that right?"

"Yes, Mrs. Davison," replied Liv.

"Oh, you must call me Philomena," she protested, leading them through an enormous bedroom furnished with antiques. She marched on to a tiny hallway at the far side of the room and opened another door, and turned on a light.

Frederica gasped, and Liv gave a low whistle. They were in a closet, as large as the bedroom and lined with wardrobe doors and built-in chests of drawers. In the center of the room, padded benches, chairs and garment racks formed an outward-facing oval, with a small sofa at each end. The fronts of the wardrobe doors were mirrored, and full-length mirrors mounted on stands were placed every few feet. Several ladies at once could admire themselves as they dressed. Makeup and hair-dressing tables completed the fitted furniture.

Philomena walked straight to a dress form, stood beside it and beamed. "I think the perfect style for two young ladies is the polonaise gown," she said, running a hand lovingly down the sleeve of a golden yellow dress printed with pink carnations and lacy greenery. Except for the long sleeves, it looked like something Cinderella might have worn to the ball.

"It used to fit me. Can you believe it?" Philomena chuckled and placed her hands on her ample waistline, then pointed to a silver-framed picture on a dressing table. In the photo, a thinner and younger version of herself wore the gown, arms linked with another young woman in a similar dress with multicolored flowers on a white background.

"Let's get to it, girls."

Philomena began to fluff out the skirt of the dress. Liv was intrigued by its design. The front was gathered at the waist and draped gracefully to the floor, while the back trailed at least a yard. "Watch this," said Philomena. She pulled two cords at the hem, and three large poufs appeared, making the skirt stand out at the hips and rear.

She pointed to Liv. "With your dark hair, I think the yellow one's for you. Frederica's fair coloring will be a perfect match for the pink-and-green-on-white." She busied herself pulling the dress out of a wardrobe and then handed it to Frederica. "Call me when you're ready for buttoning up," she said and left them alone to change.

"How do I look?" asked Liv, twirling around and holding out her long skirt, trying to catch a glimpse of the twin bustles behind.

"Perfect. Like the valance of a giant curtain escaped and attached itself to your backside."

Liv giggled. "Yeah well, you look like you could upholster a sofa just by sitting on it."

Philomena reentered without knocking and continued talking as if she'd never left. "Authentic dress gowns would have been silk de chine, of course, with hand-painted flowers. But cotton chintz yard goods for curtains work just fine." She began to fasten a long row of buttons at the back of Liv's canary-yellow and blue dress.

"And the real gowns would have had very tiny cinched waists and required serious corsets. Be grateful I put comfort before fashion."

Chapter Twenty-two

Liv and Frederica thanked Philomena and waved goodbye from their cab as it pulled away. All that effort spent pretending to be friends seemed to have taken a toll on Frederica. Her scowl thwarted the driver's attempts at pleasant conversation, and they rode most of the way back to South Kensington in silence.

Fine, thought Liv, stiffening her shoulders and exhaling loudly. *Who wants to talk to her anyway?*

As the cab drove past Kensington Park, Liv was reminded of Sir Nevil and the slippery Cumpston. Exactly how would they carry out their mission to stop Cumpston?

She stole a look at Frederica, who ran her hands through her hair and lifted her chin toward Liv. "I've thought it over," she said, "trying to decide how close we want to be to Flamsteed House when we, er, travel." Her tone was flat, matter-of-fact.

"Who put you in charge?" asked Liv.

"I did," she replied with exaggerated patience. "Do you want to pick a fight, or will you listen to my plan?"

Liv stifled the urge to strangle her and shrugged. "I'm listening."

"Here's my thinking. The party should get underway by half-past eight and may keep going strong until well after ten." She counted off her statements on her fingers.

"We can't travel to or from Greenwich at night—we'd want to be back here no later than about five in the afternoon. I think we can make the switch around noon, hide out, and sneak up to Flamsteed early. It's bound to be crawling with extra servants. If we're lucky, no one will notice us."

The cab came to a stop in front of the Havard house, and Frederica paid the driver. They made their way up the front steps, the borrowed dresses draped across their arms.

Frederica continued, "We'll hide out, do what must be done, and return with time to spare. Or do you have a better idea?"

"No," admitted Liv.

"Good. Now, let's put on our cheerful act for the parents. You only have to do it while they're watching."

"Fine by me."

The evening spent in Frederica's company was bearable. Liv ignored her moody silences punctuated with barbed comments. To her surprise, Frederica loosened up a little and even smiled a few times. It wasn't much of a performance, but it seemed to convince the Wescott and Havard parents, who had gathered for dinner, that all four young people might enjoy a day of hanging out together.

Frederica's parents were satisfied with a vague, "Oh, we'll just go here and there, probably over to Greenwich. Should be back by six." But Liv's parents wanted an itinerary, and she didn't know where to begin.

Frederica came to the rescue, rattling off descriptions of the Royal Naval College, the Maritime Museum, Greenwich Park and the Observatory like a travel brochure. "We'll visit the Queen's House and check on the rebuilding of the Cutty Sark," Frederica explained to Mrs. Wescott.

"Well, I'm delighted that you four have hit it off, and your day sounds wonderful." Mrs. Wescott rose quickly from her seat at the Havards' kitchen table to pull Anna's hands from Baxter's water dish.

"Anna and I will have Girls' Day tomorrow. We'll go to a playground, eat lunch out, then sneak home early to catch up on our napping." She rose and hoisted the diaper bag to her shoulder.

"And you big kids think you have all the adventures."

Chapter Twenty-three

"I'm hungry," said Anthony. I don't want to face the next several hours without food." They were in Greenwich. It was eleven o'clock—a little early for lunch—but Anthony was always ready to eat.

Liv offered, "How about that eel and pie shop? It's just up the street."

Cal made gagging sounds and pointed a finger to his open mouth.

Frederica laughed. "You can get other food there, Cal. This is a tourist town, and they know eel isn't to everyone's taste."

Liv led the group through the open door of the eatery, right up to the counter. Frederica whispered, "I'm off to the loo. Order anything for me but eel pie."

Anthony said, "I think I'll go, too. But the pie sounds okay." He punched Cal gently on the arm. "Order a piece for me?" Cal grimaced and nodded.

A piece of rough slate nailed to the cash register held a message: "Ask about the special." The proprietor, a thickset man with a surly expression and an apron streaked with green stains, folded his arms and glared at them.

Cal stepped forward. "May I ask about the special?"

"No, you can order or not order it—those are the choices."

"Well, I guess I'll order it then."

The man turned and looked at a dusty clock on the stucco wall. "Can't start the special until eleven thirty. It's only eleven fifteen."

"Um, okay." He squinted at the menu painted on the wall behind the man. "How about Yorkshire pudding?"

"Couldn't possibly. Just popped it into the oven. Won't be ready yet for a good long while."

"Uh, bangers and mash."

"Nope. Not a chance. The missus isn't here yet to help me with the cooking."

Cal gritted his teeth. Liv couldn't wait any longer. She said, "I'd like two orders of eel pie."

"Who's orderin' here?" the proprietor barked, uncrossing his arms and placing his hands on his hips. He turned back to Cal and waited.

Cal's shoulders dropped. "Well, all right then, let's make that three orders of eel pie."

"Not worth cutting into that lovely big pie for just three slices." He leaned over the counter conspiratorially. "Now, here's what I could do for you. I've got six Full English Breakfasts sitting in the back that I need to unload before the missus gets here for the lunch shift and sees 'em." He lowered his voice to a stage whisper. "They've gotten a bit cold, so I'll let you have 'em for half price."

"Is that our only choice?"

The man smiled. "It's either that or jellied eel with parsley liquor."

"Done!" Cal reached into a pocket with one hand and out to Liv with the other, surrendering the money from both sources.

They waited for their change and Cal scanned the walls. "What are you looking for?" whispered Liv.

"A health code rating."

"Stop making yourself conspicuous. Let's find a booth."

They sat on opposite sides of their table and scooted over to the window to leave room for the others. Anthony came back first, just as the owner appeared with a huge tray, laden with plates piled high with toast, beans, sausages and scrambled eggs. He emptied the tray and trotted back to the counter, whistling as he went.

"What—?"

"Don't ask," muttered Liv.

Costumes in their backpacks, they made their way through the streets of Greenwich, into the park and up the winding path toward the Royal Observatory, Flamsteed House.

Frederica began, "I say we go around the back of the house, away from the meridian strip and the main entrance, then duck behind some shrubs or something and put on our costumes."

"I like the part about the shrubs," said Cal. "Girls can take lookout duty while boys change, then we'll do the same for you. You two need to go last because your outfits look weirder, at least in the present." He and Anthony had bought secondhand khaki pants and long-sleeved white shirts at a charity shop, but had no luck finding used shoes that fit them. New ones were too expensive, and Liv hoped the long cuffs of the slacks would cover their running shoes.

"Over there," puffed Anthony, as they made the last turn in the uphill path. He pointed to a white service van, parked behind an imposing statue labeled *Wolfe in Winter*. It was beyond the Meridian Building and at least fifty yards from where Maskelyne would be waiting for them at the old observatory. "The van's empty. We can hide behind it, change and use the box."

Frederica looked doubtful. "That's a long distance to cover to get to Maskelyne. What if somebody stops us?"

Liv said, "Then I'll just say Sir Nevil—Uncle Nevil—is expecting us." She began to walk faster, toward the van.

"Welcome to Flamsteed House." Maskelyne greeted them in the courtyard crowded with servants carrying parcels unloaded from nearby wagons and led them to a door, where he waved them through. He raised his eyebrows and smiled. "Ah, Precious isn't among you. Excellent. Come this way."

He turned down a narrow hall. "You may remain in my apartments until time for the party." He checked his pocket-watch. "You did arrive at three o'clock, as we agreed. I value punctuality."

Anthony pointed to the timepiece in the astronomer's hand. "That looks like an H4! I've been reading all about it and about John Harrison, but I wouldn't have guessed you'd be carrying around something made by a guy you hate."

Maskelyne grinned sheepishly. "What am I to do? The miserable thing does keep the best of time."

He turned to Liv. "Now, returning to the matter at hand. His Majesty has seen fit to inform us that he will arrive with the Queen at half past eight o'clock, and he is always precisely on time. Therefore, guests must arrive before then, starting at eight." He gave a curt nod to both girls. "I shall return for the two of you shortly before eight o'clock."

"What about us?" asked Anthony.

"Well, I—I'm sure I don't know," stammered Maskelyne. "You should stay apart from the young ladies, I suppose." He pulled nervously at the cuffs of his shirt. "Don't you have some sort of plan?"

"Of course we do, Sir Nevil," said Liv, aware that it wasn't much of a plan, but not wanting to alarm him further. He seemed to fear them a little. Liv took no pleasure seeing him squirm, but someone had to be in charge.

"Attend to your duties, Sir Nevil, and don't worry about us. We'll stay right here, out of sight. Come knock on the door when you're ready, and escort us to the party." She pointed to the boys. "They'll stay in the background, ready to help if needed."

Chapter Twenty-four

It was eight forty-five. Anthony and Cal crept along the hallway, staying close to the wall. Servants in livery uniforms strode up and down the hall at a furious pace, carrying trays and receiving or barking out orders, depending on their rank.

Satisfied that no one was paying them the slightest attention, the boys inched closer to the Octagon Room entrance.

"Here! You two!" a man dressed in a scarlet coat with gold braid shouted. His white hose and polished black shoes were spotless. Only a slight soiling on his gloved fingertips and the sweat stains on his white neck scarf marred the perfection of his costume. He glanced at them, then looked away, as if they were so lowly he might contaminate himself by making eye contact. "Take these down to the kitchen."

He thrust a tray full of dirty china and wineglasses at them, turned on his heel, and returned to the Octagon Room.

"We'd better do what he says," whispered Cal. "He'll notice us if we sneak in now. Which way to the kitchen?"

"Keep your mouth shut and your head down," Anthony whispered back. Another liveried servant appeared at the end of the hall, coming toward them with a fresh tray. As they approached him, he raised his chin and made a point of ignoring them. More servants appeared, and the boys walked in the opposite direction of the procession.

A stout woman with wisps of gray hair escaping her cap and clinging to her broad face stood at the kitchen doorway. She motioned the boys past her, toward the back of the bustling room. "Well, don't just hang about—dirties that way! Shoo!" Anthony and Cal moved as directed, then stood still while a flurry of arms attacked the tray, cleared it, and handed it to a runner.

"Wait." The woman grabbed Cal by the shoulder and shoved him toward a food preparation area. "You might make yerself useful along the way." She thrust a tray of prawns at each of them and shouted, "Hand that over to one of the footmen as you go."

"We're finally headed in the right direction, at least," offered Cal.

"Yeah, but no way will any of these servers let us into the Octagon Room, and if we keep delivering trays, we could be stuck in the hallways all night. Let's hope something turns up."

The sounds of laughter, conversation and music floated down the hall. A footstep from a side passage came a millisecond before a firm hand clamped Anthony's shoulder, nearly causing him to drop the tray. A haughty voice intoned, "Hand it over and wait here. I'll return with an empty tray."

The boys waited till the man's back was turned, grinned at each other, and entered the grand Octagon Room.

Chapter Twenty-five

His Royal Highness, George the Third of England, sat on an ornate chair by the wall, beneath the wonderful year-going clocks of Thomas Tompion and huge portraits of two ancestors. He looked dumpy and plain. His simple linen coat and tired expression produced an unflattering contrast to the finery and kingly poses of Charles the Second and James the First.

Liv turned her attention from him and scanned the room. The boys were somewhere in the crowd—she'd seen them sneak in. Frederica took her by the hand and said, "Let's move about the room a bit."

They strolled around the octagonal space, and Liv was amazed that it looked no different in this time than in the present, except for the absence of electric lights. Candelabra on tall iron stands ringed the room, and the glow of fading daylight passed through the tall windows, giving everything a quality of softness. The smell of candle wax was strong, but a gentle breeze from opened windows made it bearable.

On the opposite side of the room, a small orchestra had been set up. Liv counted twelve chairs, plus a keyboard instrument with a bench. Apparently, the musicians were on break. Violins rested on velvet seats and candles on the music stands were snuffed. Liv looked around for Cumpston and spotted Maskelyne instead, bowing stiffly as he greeted his guests. She caught the astronomer's eye, and the slight shake of his head indicated that Cumpston wasn't near yet.

Liv was drawn to the keyboard and she walked over to get a better look. Was it a harpsichord? How did it feel and sound? She became aware of Frederica beside her, and they both jumped at Maskelyne's voice.

"And these are my nieces, Your Highness, the Misses Havard." Liv winced as Maskelyne took her arm and turned her firmly around to face a plump, sweet-looking older lady.

"We don't turn our backs on royalty," he hissed quietly into Liv's ear, never losing his smile or taking his eyes off the woman. Frederica immediately curtsied, and Liv followed suit. If they'd broken any rules of etiquette, the woman kindly pretended not to notice, and addressed Liv with a slight German accent that was as friendly as her smile.

"I saw you looking at the instrument with longing, my dear. It's a new fortepiano. You should play it. Go ahead—no one will mind. Enjoy yourself."

Liv's face flushed with pleasure. Permission to play a cool instrument, granted by Queen Charlotte, wife of George the Third!

She sat on the seat cushion of rich blue velvet and felt the ivory and ebony keys silently, wondering how they would respond to her touch. She plunged into her favorite Bach Invention, pleased with the delicate but beautiful tone.

Queen Charlotte beamed and nodded, making her way back to her friends and waving her hand back at Liv. Murmers of approval reached her ears before she lost herself in the joy of playing.

Polite applause followed the end of the piece, then everyone went back to partying and talking. The king had made no formal statement yet, and the guests were still abuzz with anticipation.

Liv was having fun. She began to play bits of the Mozart

sonata that she had memorized. Frederica came and went, sometimes sitting beside her and talking, then drifting off to chat with Maskelyne. There was still no sign of Cumpston or Harrison.

Deciding that no one was really paying attention to her background music, she began to play the one other thing she could remember, a favorite Beethoven sonata. She smiled as she thought how Beethoven was probably just a little child right now, and didn't notice the man making his way toward her, impatiently darting through the crowd.

"What the devil was that?" he demanded, pulling up a chair beside the harpsichord's gilded bench. "The one before sounded like that little Austrian monkey, Mozart, and never mind how a young lady like you got hold of it." He stabbed the air with his finger. "But that last one is extraordinary! I've never heard such. Whoever is the composer?"

"I'm, uh. . .visiting from America." Could she talk her way out of this? "I, er, don't have the music. A friend showed it to me. I'll have to ask her about it when I get back—to America, that is."

Frederica walked past and whispered in Liv's ear, "Brilliant! You're creating a diversion. Keep it up." Liv watched her make her way back to Maskelyne, and stood to follow.

"Wait!" the man cried. He walked a few steps to an orchestra chair and picked up a violin. Back at the fortepiano, he played a snatch of the piece. "Isn't that how it goes? What was the next part? Can you hum it for me?"

Liv was worried now. Would this man remember the tune for a long time? When Beethoven wrote it later, would there be a lawsuit? She reached for the keys and began to repeat one of her earlier selections, ignoring the man until he shrugged and walked away.

She became aware of a plain brown jacket, its elbows at her eye level. She'd gotten used to people wandering by, murmuring compliments or just listening for a moment before moving on. She wondered what this one would say. She glanced up at his face, then wished she hadn't. It was the king.

Calm down, she told herself. He must be enjoying it.

King George smiled. "I recall a time when a little boy—young Mozart—came to London and played for us," he said wistfully. "He ran around in the palace garden with my children and sat on my wife Charlotte's lap." He sighed and wiped his eyes. "It was a happy time. My own children loved me. Even the colonies, my American 'children', loved me. Or so I thought."

His shoulders sagged, and he placed a hand on the fortepiano to steady himself. "It's different now." Liv continued to play, unsure if she should say anything, but feeling an unexpected wave of sympathy for this man her country would fight to be rid of in a few years.

She knew the music so well that she could continue playing and look beyond him. No more than ten feet away, Frederica was nodding at Maskelyne and beginning to make her way toward Cumpston, who had just stepped into the room.

Cumpston snapped his fingers at a servant carrying a tray of wineglasses and took two without thanking him, holding them both in one hand. If Liv hadn't been looking for suspicious behavior, she would never have noticed that Cumpston moved his palm over one glass, then took it in his free hand and swirled it around.

Maskelyne was now speaking earnestly to a man who must be John Harrison, pursuing him while Harrison attempted to break away. But the farther Harrison moved from Maskelyne, the closer he came to Cumpston, and to Liv and the king. Obviously not eager to converse with his rival of many years, Harrison turned toward the smiling Cumpston and inclined his head, falling for the "rescue".

"Forgive me, Your Majesty, but you have to move." She stood up and pulled at George's sleeve. Cumpston and Harrison came closer, and she saw Cumpston reaching into his pocket. "Now!"

"You don't touch a king!" cried Frederica, suddenly appearing at Liv's side as the monarch raised his eyebrows and peered down at Liv in disapproval.

Frederica turned from Liv and the king and stepped in front of Cumpston. "Don't do it, Mr. Cumpston. You'll be caught and hanged for it."

Cumpston's eyes widened, then narrowed as recognition slowly dawned. "You two!" He checked the wineglasses, took a sip from the one that wasn't cloudy, and set them down on an orchestra chair. "I assure you, I won't be caught, as my preparations are meticulous. But since you've rather spoiled my first plan, I'll put the second one into play." He pulled a pistol from inside his jacket, keeping it half-hidden by the jacket and covering the barrel with a silk kerchief.

"No!" cried Liv and Frederica, but their voices were lost in the sounds of the party. Cumpston aimed the pistol at Harrison, who was focused on Liv, pushing forward to protect the king from her and politely requesting that His Majesty step back a bit. The pop of the gun went unnoticed, sounding more like the uncorking of a champagne bottle than an assassin's bullet.

Liv held her breath and waited for Harrison to fall while the king, with a puzzled look on his face, put a finger to his side. He stared at the red stain that appeared there, growing quickly to the size of a grapefruit.

John Harrison had stepped forward to shield the king, and had caused him to move into Cumpston's line of fire.

Chapter Twenty-six

The girls watched in horrified fascination as the monarch sat heavily on the floor and was immediately surrounded by a swarm of would-be helpers. Men shouted, a woman screamed, and Liv grabbed Frederica's arm. "Find Cumpston! Where is he?"

"He's gone! I don't see him anywhere!"

Liv looked around the room and caught Anthony's eye. Anthony grabbed Cal's arm and headed toward the door. Liv nodded and did the same with Frederica.

Fighting their way against the tide of people rushing toward the king, the four reached the doorway at the same time and squeezed out together, spilling into the hall. Cal, athletic and not wearing a long dress, took the lead. The girls picked up their skirts and followed, trailed by Anthony.

Around a corner they ran, down a flight of stairs. "Any sign of Cumpston?" puffed Liv.

Cal stopped at the bottom of the stairs and looked in every direction. "None. I don't know which way to go, and it's too dangerous to split up right now."

Frederica and Anthony caught up, and Frederica took the

lead. "Let's head to the front, toward the path downhill."

They scurried to an outside door and onto a small stone stoop, lit feebly by a black iron lantern nailed to the masonry. Liv gave a little shriek as a man cried, "There you are!"

It was her musician friend, on his way back in and unaware of the drama going on inside Flamsteed House. "I wasn't finished questioning you! What about—"

Liv grabbed both his forearms to get his attention. "Did you see a man running away? Heavyset with a green velvet jacket, thick lips? He's committed a crime!"

"A woman very nearly knocked me down just now—right over there!" He pointed into the darkness.

"The odd thing was her shoes. They were men's shoes. I couldn't see her face—she wore a veil."

He looked at Liv. "That was your man, wasn't it?" He shook his head. "You'll never find him now." He started up the stairs. "I must get back to the party."

"There's no more—" began Frederica.

Liv caught her arm and whispered, "He'll find out soon, and we want to be long gone before he tells someone we were running away and asking about the murderer."

The man had barely disappeared inside the entrance when Cal said, "We can't let Cumpston get away! I'm a pretty good sprinter—let me make a quick circle around the grounds."

Frantic to keep the group together, Liv said, "The damage is already done. And don't forget, I was with the king when it happened. Frederica was right there, too." She looked up at the brightly lit windows. "They may come looking for him and us any second."

No sooner had she finished than they heard muffled shouts from inside, and the door burst open.

Cal nodded. "Quick!" he whispered. "Let's move over to that tree. If we time travel right here, we'll be standing on the Prime Meridian and all the tourists will see us." He raced ten yards and stopped. The others followed. "Hold on to me," he panted.

Cal's fingers were quick, and it took only seconds for him

to open the box and set the drawers properly. Still, before the positioning was complete, a voice cried out, "There they are! Over there!"

They locked arms and closed their eyes.

Chapter Twenty-seven

With no time passing in the present, they would appear in full daylight. Liv hoped the tourist crowd would be focused on the brass strip with the red LED printout that marked zero degrees longitude, and so fail to notice the peculiar-looking foursome.

But there was no crowd. The spacious brick-paved area in front of the observatory was planted with grass, and the only access to the building was a narrow gravel path. "Look, guys," said Anthony. "It's gone."

He was right. The dividing line between the Eastern and Western hemispheres, the Prime Meridian, was nowhere to be seen. Not knowing what else to do, they walked up to the entry and stood as Liv read aloud the words on the brass plaque beside the door.

"Flamsteed House, constructed sixteen seventy-five to sixteen seventy-six, partly of recycled materials, and paid for by the sale of decayed gunpowder at a cost of five hundred twenty pounds. Residence of many Astronomers Royal.

"After the assassination of King George the Third, champion of John Harrison's H4 timepiece, which made possible the determination of longitude at sea, and the ensuing madness of Royal Astronomer Sir Nevil Maskelyne, England's prominence in that science was threatened. In eighteen eighty-four, the official Prime Meridian of the world was declared to be in Paris, France."

"Let's go," said Anthony, his face pale. "We can decide what to do while we walk back."

"I've had just about enough of this dress," complained Liv as she hiked her skirts up for the third time with one hand, holding her shoes in the other, and grimacing at each piece of gravel that dug into the soles of her feet.

"Well, stop sweating in it!" Frederica ordered. "I'm sure it's had enough of you, too, and Philomena won't be happy about getting it back all smelly."

Anthony gazed down the hill at the city of Greenwich below. "We have a long way to go. We can slow down now. Nobody's chasing us." He shook his head sympathetically. "Too bad you couldn't bring a change of clothes."

Frederica giggled. "Oh, but we did." She pointed to the bustle-like poufs below the waist of her gown. "You can pack quite a bit in here. T-shirts and flip-flops, for instance. We never took off our shorts, so we need only a moment to change. I say we stop at the first available place with a loo."

Liv offered, "That would probably be a sandwich shop. I'm betting Anthony scoped out all of them."

"Of course," he replied.

They made their way along the path, flanked by huge sweet Spanish chestnut trees, alive with birds and butterflies. A large sign with arrows pointed the ways to cricket, rugby, tennis and putting areas. "Hmm. . ." said Frederica, "I don't see much difference in the park. That's good."

An audience was gathering for a puppet show, while a group of determined-looking individuals, some armed with garden spades, waited beside a sign reading, "Plant Sale and Practical Demonstration: Propagation of Herbaceous Perennials".

"Normal," observed Frederica. "Absolutely normal."

They arrived in the town and walked two by two on the sidewalk, ignoring the stares of passersby and the requests of tourists to stop and have their pictures taken with them. Anthony took the lead, looking ahead, turning onto King William Street, where he stopped at last in front of a shop called Nauticalia.

"I knew it would be like this," he said. "I just had to see it with my own eyes."

"See what?" asked Liv. "It looks the same to me."

"When we passed it before, the sign was different. It said, 'First Shop in the World' with the longitude marking—almost zero degrees."

Liv put her hand on Anthony's shoulder. "We need to go home. We're going to have to do something, and I don't even know where to start."

Chapter Twenty-eight

"So, you're saying Cumpston was never caught for George's assassination? Let's hope he was too scared to follow through with killing Harrison." Liv waited for Frederica's reply.

She watched idly as Anthony and Cal threw a baseball back and forth. They'd brought their gloves along to Kensington Park this morning, to pass the time while they waited for Frederica. Now she was here, but they weren't quite ready to stop. Frederica remained silent, and Liv shifted uncomfortably on the park bench. An unspoken truce had developed since the girls' first trip to Greenwich, and Liv wanted it to last, at least as long as they needed Frederica's help. After that. . .who could tell?

Among other things was the issue of Frederica's cutting. Liv suspected the little cuts might have been for shock value. She'd known Liv would come to her room, looking for her backpack, and she'd left the door open.

But the scars higher up on her arms—those were evidence of something much more serious. Since that first day, Frederica hadn't spoken a word about cutting, and more often than not, she'd been pleasant.

It was almost like being friends, except that friends, Liv knew, would talk about their problems. A good friend would listen and try to help. Liv wasn't sure she was ready to be anyone's good friend.

The boys wandered over, laughing and trading insults with each other. Cal made it to the bench first, ball in hand. Liv cupped both hands together and held them out. Cal tossed the ball to her, and she pitched it to Anthony. He caught it, kept jogging toward them, and threw it back.

The ball headed for the park bench, and Frederica squealed and jumped out of the way. Liv caught it easily and said, "My brother isn't the world's greatest pitcher, but he's not that bad. Here," she said, holding out the ball to Frederica, "you try it."

Instead of making a haughty refusal, Frederica took the ball and threw it. Her pitch fell short, and Anthony scrambled to pick it up and throw it back.

Frederica appeared to be trying hard, arms outstretched. She missed the ball, and refused to attempt another throw. "I don't know what you Americans see in that silly game." She sounded aloof, but Liv noticed the skin in the V of her T-shirt starting to get blotchy.

Cal scooped up the ball from the grass, and Anthony said, "We're ready to get down to business if you are. Got any bright ideas?"

The red spots began to fade, and Frederica sniffed, "It seems rather simple to me. We just go back again to yesterday—same time—and watch for Cumpston to arrive. We tell a guard or someone that he has a pistol. That we saw him take it out of his coat pocket."

"Won't work." Anthony pulled off his glove and stared into the distance, as if he'd just given up on Frederica as a source of help.

"Well, I can't think why not!" Her pale face flushed and the blotches returned. "We did see him do it—the fact that it won't have happened yet doesn't matter."

She waved a hand in front of Anthony's face to get his attention. "If he's caught and searched, they'll find the gun, and maybe the poison, too."

She scanned their faces. "Why are you all looking at me that way? At least it's a plan, which is more than I've heard from any of you." She turned to Liv. "If you've a better idea, now's the time to say so."

Liv exhaled, puffing out her cheeks. "It's not a bad idea, Frederica. The trouble is, we don't know how to control anything but the year. If we go back today, we'd arrive the day after the assassination."

"Oh."

Anthony said, "So, to state the obvious, we can't afford to wait a whole year for the big day to come around again. The three of us won't be in London."

"I don't have a plan, guys, but I'm pretty sure of two things," said Liv. The others waited. She took a deep breath and began.

"First, we have to go back to the year before all this happens—seventeen seventy-one.

"Second, we're in over our heads. I think you boys had better see about contacting your friend Morehouse. He seems like a good one to have on our side, and we need all the help we can get."

"No, no-o-o," Cal groaned, holding his head and lowering it between his knees. Anthony grimaced and frowned.

"Besides," she continued, as if she hadn't seen them, "he knows this crowd. Cumpston was the one who stalked Morehouse, at the king's request. He was supposed to have killed him."

"What?" Cal's head shot upright, his hands still over his ears. "How do you know that, and why didn't you tell us?" he demanded.

"I meant to—I really did. It just slipped my mind, with everything else that was going on." She looked at the boys. They didn't seem to be buying it.

"Okay," she conceded, "that was partly true. At first, I just didn't have the nerve to mention it. Later, I did actually forget about it."

Cal blew out a sigh. Anthony threw his baseball glove on the grass and sat down beside it.

Frederica pointed to Liv. "Be mad at her if you like, but I think she's right, as long as this Morehouse is trustworthy. He's comfortable in the seventeen-seventies—we're not. He knows the place and the people, he's an adult, and don't forget. . ." She leaned back on the bench and crossed her arms. "He already knows the secret of your time-travel box. You wouldn't be letting anyone else in on it."

Cal looked at Anthony. "Who's going to meet with him?"

"The four of us," Liv replied firmly.   "We're in this together."

Chapter Twenty-nine

"What do you mean, you can't find it?" Liv tried not to shout, but she could hear her voice rise in pitch.

Anthony shook his head, and Cal looked nervously toward the bedroom of their apartment, where Anna and her parents were still sleeping. It was seven o'clock in the morning, and they wouldn't be alone much longer.

Liv picked up Anthony's wallet from an end table and began taking everything out, searching for Morehouse's business card. "You don't need your Adelaide Village library card over here, you know," she said, sorting through the wallet's contents and shaking her head. "Or Honor Society membership, or Spanish Club. But maybe it's a good sign. You never throw anything away."

She pointed to the coat closet. "Have you checked all your pockets?"

"No, and I can't right now—I have to put all this stuff back in my wallet."

Anthony picked up his belongings and began methodically restoring them to his version of order, his mouth set in a grim expression.

Liv rolled her eyes and Cal shuffled over from the sleeper sofa they had just reopened to search.

"I'll dig through the pockets," he said. "Go make nice to your brother. We won't be very productive if you two are bickering all day."

Liv turned and walked back to Anthony. "Sorry," she said. "The card is pretty small, and you didn't have a reason to think you needed to keep up with it. It's nothing compared to what I let get away from me." Her eyes filled with tears, and she picked up the rest of Anthony's cards and held them out.

Anthony smiled and punched her gently on the shoulder. It was good to have a brother who pretended not to notice the tears.

"Ha!" Cal closed the closet door and ran back to them, holding the small white card and waving it.

He passed the card to Anthony and asked, "Who gets to make the call?"

"Not me," said Liv. "I never met the man till we saw him at the airport."

"Not me," echoed Cal. "I'm not good under pressure."

Liv turned to her Brother and smiled. "Anthony can handle this. What do you say, brother?" It might not make up for snapping at him, or for not telling them about old Cumpston's connection to Morehouse, but Anthony seemed to appreciate the vote of confidence and nodded, tucking the card into his wallet.

"We can't call from here," he said. "It's too early, and we couldn't explain the phone charge to Mom and Dad. We could look for a pay phone, but it'd be better to get your new best friend Frederica to let us use her cell phone."

Liv snorted. "How about 'worst friend'? 'Frenemy'?"

She stopped. "Though, you know, she's gotten about fifteen percent less obnoxious lately. At the rate she's going, she could be almost human in a few decades."

Cal spoke up. "I think you need to lighten up on her a little. She seems kind of okay. Maybe she just needs someone to like her for who she is."

"Yeah, an obnoxious, egotistical brat—"

Anthony finished her sentence. "—who outsmarted you. And now she's trying to help us."

He touched Liv's arm. "So let her help."

It was later in the day, at Liv's official piano practice time, that she and the boys arrived at the Havards' house. Liv's backpack held her music, stacked on top of the box. Anthony and Cal had brought their gloves, and they tossed the baseball back and forth while Liv rang the doorbell. They were greeted, as usual, by Baxter, who took a particular interest in the gloves, whining and wagging his tail.

Upstairs, Mrs. Havard exclaimed, "Oh, Liv, you've brought an audience with you—how lovely!" Then, when she saw the baseball, "Sorry, boys, that definitely looks like an outside activity. You'd better head to the nearest park. That would be Kensington."

"We're on our way, Mrs. Havard," said Anthony. "But we thought we'd see if Frederica wanted to come." He reached into Liv's backpack and pulled out his dad's well-worn glove as Mrs. Havard's eyes widened in surprise.

"Well, best of luck to you, but I think the chances of Rica's wanting to play baseball are somewhere between improbable and impossible."

A red streak sailed across the kitchen and soared through the transom above the door to the dining room. It was followed seconds later by a green one, squawking, "Pretty bird! Pretty bird!"

"What you might do," she continued, not even looking up, "is talk her into taking a walk with those two. It seems we've acquired a foster macaw."

Cal ignored Liv's horror-struck expression. "I guess we could," he volunteered, some doubt evident in his voice. "Do they have little collars with leashes?"

"Oh, they do indeed, though McGinty's never tried to fly off on his own when we take him out. It's Precious I don't trust."

She sighed. "It looks like we've gotten ourselves another pet. McGinty is absolutely smitten with her, and no one has answered our adverts."

She leaned toward them and stage-whispered, "Just between us, I think that bird resided in a tavern. Her language is as colorful as her feathers."

"Auraw-w-k! Pour me another one!" Precious screamed.

"You might want to keep away from children while you've got her out. Oh, here, I'm talking as if you'd already agreed to walk them."

McGinty appeared in the transom space and perched, locking his eyes on Liv while his irises expanded and contracted.

"I'll just run back and say hi to Frederica," Liv said, moving as quickly as possible toward the bedrooms.

"And thanks again for calling Mrs. Davison, uh, Philomena, for us. We had a wonderful time." Liv didn't mention that the dresses had looked a little worse for the wear after their adventure, and were now at the dry cleaner.

She walked down the hall and eyed the half-open door to Frederica's room, remembering what she had seen the first time she'd entered it. She knocked, and Frederica called out from the bathroom, "In here."

Liv looked all around the room. White furniture, pink rug, pink bedspread. A typical girl's room, except. . .the bed pillows were positioned perfectly. Hair clips and barrettes lined up in precise order on the dresser, like soldiers at parade rest. Makeup and lotion bottles were arranged in rows and columns. They were grouped by color and size, in order of the spectrum: pinks—large, medium, and small; beiges—ditto; then blues; and finally, whites.

On a desk, next to a cell phone in its charger, were a dozen newly-sharpened pencils laid out side by side, each one sharpened down to exactly the same length. Liv suspected that if she peeked in drawers or the wardrobe, she'd find things arranged with the same rigor.

She looked again at the pencils and couldn't resist. She shifted one slightly askew, just in time to avoid being caught by Frederica as she emerged from the bathroom.

Her pale blond hair was pulled back into a ponytail, topped by a pale blue baseball cap. Faded jeans and white flip-flops shot the paleness factor up a few more notches, in Liv's opinion, and the white, long-sleeved T-shirt sent it over the top. She looked like a ghost.

"Nice hat," managed Liv. "Grab your phone. Anthony's going to call Morehouse when the three of you get to Kensington Park and see if he'll meet with us."

Frederica nodded and removed the phone from its charger, then paused, frowning at the pencils. She straightened the offender.

"I'm ready," she said, scanning the room, as if other random objects might have jumped out of place while she wasn't looking. "Now, what was that about when you get to Kensington Park. Didn't you mean we?"

"Oh, no," said Liv. "Your mother talked the boys into taking both of your insane birds for a little walk in the park. I feel a sudden urge to practice."

"Not so fast." Frederica caught up with her before she reached the doorway and placed an arm across it, blocking her path. "I distinctly remember hearing you say we were in this together. We all heard you."

She lowered her arm and grabbed Liv by the elbow. "So stop your foot-dragging and let's get on with it. If one didn't know better, one might think the perfect Ms. Wescott had a parrot phobia."

"It's not a phobia. You may have a few—I just have a perfectly normal aversion to anyone who stares at me and makes his pupils grow and shrink really fast. What did he mean by that, anyway?"

Frederica asked, "Was he spreading out his tailfeathers?"

"Yeah, I think so."

"In that case," Frederica said, "it was probably, 'I should like to kill you.' But he flashes his eyes all the time now to Precious, and it means, 'Hello, Beautiful.'"

"Great," grumbled Liv, pulling her backpack onto her shoulders. "Be sure you keep her in his line of sight all the time, because I can't be responsible for what happens if he attacks me. I'd hate to resort to violence, but in his case I think I could make an exception."

Downstairs, Mrs. Havard left the house for an orchestra rehearsal, and Frederica removed Baxter's leash from a hook on the wall.

"Want to go with us?" she asked. Baxter replied by way of wagging the entire back half of his body, struggling to hold himself still enough to have the leash attached to his collar.

Then Frederica whistled, and the sound of flapping wings, punctuated by squawks, filled the room. McGinty and Precious settled in on Frederica's shoulders, and she winced as they gripped with their toes. Baxter turned his head and cocked it, narrowing his eyes and giving a barely audible growl.

As the four humans and two avians made their way to the door, it seemed to occur to Baxter that the house was about to be bird-free for awhile, and he turned and ran back down the hall, straining to get traction on the wood floor and trailing his leash behind him.

"I'll just run and fetch him," offered Liv.

"Leave him," Frederica ordered. "I don't trust you to come back."

"That's insulting!" Liv turned to her brother. "Do I have to let her talk to me like that?"

Anthony shrugged. "You two want to butt heads or get something done?"

Liv sighed and fell into step with Cal, behind Anthony and Frederica. With a one-hundred-eighty degree turn of his head, McGinty gave Liv a full-on stare, then slowly blinked one eye.

He wasn't just a menace. He was a smart-aleck.

Chapter Thirty

"Wish me luck," Anthony murmured, looking at the phone number on Morehouse's business card and punching buttons.

Liv, Cal and Frederica watched in silence. McGinty and Precious groomed each other behind Frederica's head.

Two loud rings sounded, and Anthony said, "It's ringing, ringing. I bet it's going to go to voice mail."

Then there was a click, and a familiar voice carried loud and clear through the phone. "Morehouse here."

"Oh, man," mouthed Anthony in a low whisper.

"Who's that?"

Anthony cleared his throat. "Mr. Morehouse, this is Anthony. My friend and I ran into you in Gatwick Airport, remember? You gave us your business card?"

They all listened to Morehouse's booming reply. "Why, of course, lad! It's good to hear you again. I wanted to pass on a word of caution to you and Cal, but I hadn't got round to it, so your call is most timely."

"How do you know our names? We never told you our names."

Liv clasped and unclasped her hands, rethinking the wisdom of contacting the former pirate.

"Don't let that worry you," he said. "Or the fact that I know where you're staying. It's someone else I wanted to talk to you about, but wait—you called me. You first."

Anthony explained their situation, leaving out nothing, except for the identity of Cumpston. Liv supposed Anthony didn't want to overload Morehouse and scare him off. There was no response for several seconds, and she thought the phone might have gone dead.

Anthony wound up his speech with a plea. "We need you to go back with us and do something to stop the bad guy from killing this man—or anyone else."

The phone wasn't dead. It vibrated in Anthony's hand as Morehouse's voice roared through it. "You want me to do what?"

Anthony held the phone at arm's length as Morehouse continued his rant. "Have you collectively gone mad, or do you simply not remember that I left London in the seventeen-seventies for a very good reason?"

Liv became aware that Precious was jumping up and down on Frederica's shoulder, straining at her little bird leash and leaning toward the phone.

"Look," whispered Liv. "She's doing the eye-flash thing at the phone."

Frederica answered, "She probably just likes the color, and it's shiny."

Precious broke free and flew to Anthony's shoulder, fluttering her wings and pecking at the phone. "Are you a pirate? Are you a pirate?" she squealed.

"I know that voice!" Morehouse's own sounded disbelieving. "It's not human—it's. . .No, it couldn't be." He cleared his throat. "Back to the matter at hand, Anthony. I'll meet with you, and we'll talk. I can do it in an hour, but not at your place. My associate knows where you're staying, and these days I never know what might set him off.

"There's a lovely little eel pie and mash shop, just a short journey for you. It's called The Jellied Eel." Cal groaned and held his stomach.

Morehouse continued, "Take the tube toward Notting Hill, and the shop's in Portobello Road. Hop off at the Ladbroke Grove stop, and it's a two-minute walk for you. Got that?"

"Got it," said Anthony, and hung up. He pulled Precious from his arm and handed her to Frederica. "Let's get these two back to your place."

The four walked back, and Precious sang snatches of tunes with words like "ale" and "buccaneer." McGinty hunkered down and leaned on Frederica's cheek, looking depressed.

"Don't worry, buddy," Anthony told him. "She isn't Morehouse's type."

Chapter Thirty-one

In spite of its name, The Jellied Eel was attractive and clean. Live eels swam in tanks at the shop's front window, and a long marble countertop ran almost the length of the place. Black and white wall tiles and an abundance of mirrors complemented the Victorian wrought-iron chairs and tables, but did nothing to ensure privacy.

Liv looked left and right on the street before leading the others inside. Morehouse was waiting for them. They were close to Portobello Road Market, where Cumpston and his partners had their place of business, but surely the chances of running into him were small. Besides, Morehouse knew how to take care of himself, and he had suggested the place.

She brushed her fears aside, followed Morehouse up to the cash register, and listened as he ordered eels and mash for everyone. The others trailed along, and minutes later they were padding over the clean sawdust floor to help themselves to forks and spoons.

Cal rummaged through the silverware box. "I need a knife."

"You won't find one, mate," advised Morehouse. "A proper

pie house has no knives. Proximity to pubs and all that."

"Why is the furniture bolted to the floor?" asked Liv.

"Same reason." He carried his loaded plate to a marble-topped table in a deserted corner of the shop. He selected a hard-backed wooden seat and motioned to the others to do the same.

The boys set their plates on either side of him and the girls sat at the next table, swiveling their chairs to face the others.

Anthony immediately began consuming his feast while Cal and the girls stared at the mounds on their plates.

"Come on, tuck in," ordered Morehouse. "You're looking at a time-honored delicacy. Londoners have been eating eels for thousands of years." He picked up a large bottle of malt vinegar and sprinkled it liberally over his plate.

"In ancient times, you just walked down to the river and caught, cooked and ate your eel. The jellied eel stalls in the Middle Ages were a great invention." He smiled at the thought. "Washed down with a pint—a sweeter meat you've never tasted."

Liv pulled a sliver of meat from the spiny bones with her fork, then loaded her spoon with mashed potatoes. She buried the meat in a mouthful of potato and swallowed without chewing. Congratulating herself, she repeated the process. Frederica watched for a moment, then tried the same thing.

Cal took a bite of meat, closed his eyes, swallowed quickly, and made a face. A shudder began at his mouth and traveled down his entire body.

"Okay," he said to no one in particular. "I tried it. Are you happy?"

Anthony spoke with his mouth full. "And you're not going to finish it? I can't believe you—this stuff is great!" He reached for the bottle of vinegar. "Here," he said, drenching Cal's plate with the liquid, "you need more of this. Or just spoon some of that crazy green sauce on it. What's not to like?"

"What's in the sauce?"

Morehouse wiped his mouth with a paper napkin. "It's just the water from the pot used to cook the eels. They boil parsley in it to give the lovely green color we call it parsley liquor."

Cal pushed his plate away and looked out the window.

Frederica laughed. "It's okay, Cal. I don't like them either. The bones stick out like thumbtacks, and you have to chew and chew that slimy skin. The jelly's the worst part of it—like someone with a sinus infection had a great sneeze."

"You're not helping!" he said, keeping his face toward the window. Something on the street seemed to capture his attention, and he laid his fork down and stared.

When he turned back to the others, he whispered to Morehouse, "It's lucky you made me look out there. Two guys are standing on the corner." He stole a glance. "They were looking right at us and now they're talking to each other, but they're still not moving."

"Mmm. . .it's Nigel and Eddie—two of Lance's toughs," Morehouse said in an undertone. "They're not the sharpest rounds of cheese in the cheddar factory. Usually they just deliver messages for Lance, which I suspect come with threats and a bit of roughing up."

He spooned a bite of mashed potatoes and swallowed. "But why hang about out there, watching us and not coming in? I don't like it." As he spoke, the two nodded at each other and moved on.

"Probably nothing to worry about," said Morehouse, "but it bears being a little more careful. We won't come here again."

Chapter Thirty-two

It was time to get down to it. Frederica began, smiling at Morehouse. "The others tell me you were something of a buccaneer in your day."

"Well, I suppose I was for a time," he admitted, a hint of pride showing in his voice. "My usefulness, in the government's opinion, was attacking French East India Company ships. It drove the company out of business in seventeen sixty-nine. As a reward, I was offered the position of lieutenant on a British East India Company vessel with the promise of working my way up to captain, but I turned it down."

He leaned back and crossed his arms. "Now there was a magnificent ship—a British East Indiaman. Lord of the Ocean. It couldn't outrun a pirate ship, mind you, but it took care of itself with heavy arms."

Anthony was wide-eyed. "It sounds awesome—what an adventure! How come you turned it down?"

"It was dangerous enough. But adventure? Back and forth, back and forth, officer cabins furnished like a fancy house, crews with scurvy, dysentery, and the likes of me chasing after them." He shook his head. "No thanks, I told them, I'll just keep on pirating. Things began to go downhill, to use a modern expression, after that."

His voice turned bitter. "We'd served the government for over a century, mapping the Caribbean, collecting scientific data, harassing the Spanish Navy." He stabbed at his potatoes. "Why, there was a time when whole towns in the Caribbean made their livelihood by trading with pirate crews like mine, buying our booty and selling us supplies."

Anthony whistled softly.

"Often my crew and I pretended to steal goods from the merchants, when we were actually paying—double price, in fact. Dealers would leave things 'unattended,' then send a messenger to collect the money and tell us where to find them. And I can tell you, the officials and legal merchants often behaved worse than the pirates, so I chose my side. We were democratic—no matter what your race, religion or prior social rank—if you were on the ship, you had a vote." He smiled at the memory.

"By the time I got into the life, the British government's imperialist takeover of the Caribbean and South Pacific was almost complete. The state turned its back on my kind, criminalizing and imprisoning us. They couldn't hire me or convince me to turn in my fellow privateers, so I became a liability to be disposed of at all cost."

He propped his elbows on the table. "So, you can understand, London in seventeen seventy-two would be the last place I'd want to go. And I must ask, why me?"

"We're in situation that's beyond us," said Frederica, giving the others a look that dared them to say otherwise. "We need someone with connections, experience and intelligence. No one alive can match your combination of those qualities."

He looked pleased. "And exactly what is it you need done that only I can do?"

Liv spoke up. "We've tried to think of several possibilities, Mr. Morehouse, and we hoped you might have some ideas of your own."

Morehouse picked up his fork, snorted, and took another

bite. Liv continued, "It's the twelfth of June today. King George the Third was assassinated on June eleventh. We don't know how to choose the month or day when we travel, just the year. So do it today, and you go on the twelfth of June. The closest you can get is seventeen-seventy-one almost a year before the event.

"We were hoping you could draw Cumpston away from the scene—maybe offer him something to disappear, or send him on a really long errand out of the country—even kidnap him. Anything—just so it takes him months and months to get back home."

Morehouse dropped his fork and stopped chewing his eel pie. "Who's that? What was the name? I didn't know any Cumpston in the seventies—the seventeen seventies, that is."

"Well, he knows all about you!" said Cal. "Or knew about you. He had you followed. He was paid by the king to make you disappear, and he hired the guy who gave you your scar."

Morehouse gave his parsley liquor a languid stir. "Even after all this time, it's daunting to learn the name of the person who pursued me and tried to carry out His Majesty's orders to kill me. It gives me a bad feeling about Lance, too. Heredity or environment, he seems to have continued the family tradition. And now I've two descendants of men from my past to deal with."

"Two?" Liv's discomfort increased. Morehouse surely had some strange baggage.

Chapter Thirty-three

"Jonathan Pridgeon was my Quartermaster in the sixties—the seventeen-sixties," Morehouse said, "and a finer one I never saw. He was my second-in-command, elected by the crew, though I would have chosen him myself. He kept order on the ship, settled disputes kept records, and fought alongside me every time."

The memory brought a smile to Morehouse's face. "He led a raid on a Spanish ship, which we decided to keep. He wanted to take a few crew members and become captain of it, and I was happy to reward him for years of faithful service. Pridgeon headed to Jamaica and recruited enough British sailors to desert the navy and fill out his crew.

"Imagine my surprise when I first stepped into Carmine's office and saw the oil painting on the wall behind his desk. Jonathan's ship, which he renamed the *Blue Star*, with him at the helm! I nearly swallowed my tongue—I'd never made the connection, in spite of the uncommonness of the name."

Morehouse peered out the window and cut his eyes left and right. Satisfied, he returned to his story. "He'd bought the painting because it had his ancestor in it, but he'd never heard of me, which was a great relief. I suppose it lulled me into complacency to know a descendant of my good friend was one of those in charge, and I didn't look into the firm's doings as I should have. Jonathan would never have let things get out of hand like this."

He shook his head. "It pains me to say it, but Carmine is more corruptible than his ancestor ever was."

Frederica asked, "More corruptible than a pirate?"

The handsome smile froze. "You see yourself as better than imperialists of your own time? Better than other pirates of my time who joined the government to rid itself of pirate competition?" Morehouse lowered his voice to a growl. "I find it incredibly offensive that anyone would compare what wealthy colonists did to Africans, indigenous peoples, women, natural resources—even their own working classes to what I did in my pirate prime."

He returned to his eel pie and chewed thoughtfully. "Sure, I captured and held for ransom occasionally, but only people who could afford to pay. And I hardly ever resold."

"You sold some people twice?" Cal squeaked. Morehouse waved him off and shrugged.

"I had no right to speak to you that way," said Frederica. She held her head high, but her voice quivered. "I'm the one who stole the box from Liv and started this mess."

"Maybe so, Frederica, but the box was in my care," said Liv miserably. "I let everyone down."

Morehouse looked to the boys, who suddenly seemed very interested in their food. Cal picked bits of eel meat from the spiky bones and sank them in the pool of parsley liquor nestled in a mound of mashed potatoes. Anthony stared at his near-empty plate.

The pirate sighed and ran a hand through his wavy, dark hair. "There's enough blame to go around for all, but right now we've work to do. Allow me to recap and see if I understand. I'm expected to save one of my mortal enemies—Cumpston—from killing another mortal enemy—the King himself—all at the request of you two blighters and your friends here. I should have sold you off when I first met you."

Anthony spoke up. "Well, no offense, Mr. Morehouse, but that's exactly what you tried to do. It just didn't work out."

Morehouse laughed. "You're a pair, aren't you? And what if I don't want to save His Royal Highness? He wasn't much of a friend to me. And Cumpston?"

Anthony slapped his hand on the table and ignored the "Shh!" from Liv.

"That's exactly what I'm starting to think," he said. "I did a little research before we left home, reading about George the Third and some other monarchs, scoping out what I might want to see while we're here. Did you know he had a disease that made him crazy and miserable when he was old? Maybe it isn't up to us to decide who would be better off dead, but it looks like America still got its independence even with George being killed. What about the American and British soldiers who wouldn't have to die, if reasonable heads prevailed and cut the war short? Maybe we should just leave things the way they are now."

Morehouse shook his head. "The king was no friend to me, but I won't decide when he should die. And let the revolution take its course. America will have to go down the path it chose."

He set his empty plate on Anthony's and lifted his tray, motioning for Anthony to slide his own beneath it. "It's still my opinion this time traveling business is wrong, mind you, but I'm beginning to think it might be fun to pull one over on old Cumpston. I find it hard to worry about the lasting effects on him and his descendants, knowing one of them as I do."

He looked at them one by one. "Now, the question is: Where to send him? This must be carefully thought out."

He rose from his chair and led the way to the tray return area, sorting out plates utensils, and trash as the others handed him their trays. "We'll have Cumpston abducted and sent to. . . the Caribbean, I think. Barbados? Nevis? Antigua?"

"Maskelyne's been to Barbados," said Liv. "I don't think he liked it much."

"Then, Barbados has possibilities!"

A thud and a scuffling of footsteps sounded behind them, and they turned to see a busboy speeding away, ponytail bouncing on the back of his neck and plastic dishpan carelessly tossed on a table.

Morehouse grimaced. "Apparently the walls have ears in this place. Let's walk a bit, shall we?"

Chapter Thirty-four

They exited the shop and followed Morehouse down an alley. "Sorry not to treat you to a tour," he said, "but we need privacy. Now, it may take several hours in the past—even a whole day—to set up everything for Octavius Cumpston. One of you needs to come along to take me, bring me back and act as general dogsbody while we're there. Who's going then? Cal?"

"I guess I can." Cal shifted his weight from one foot to another.

"I know I can," Anthony said. "Take both of us."

"Done," said Morehouse.

Anthony pulled the box from the pocket of his jacket, and Morehouse turned to the girls. "We'll be right back."

Liv said to Frederica, "Keep an eye out in all directions. They may not pop up exactly where they left."

There was no time to watch or worry. Morehouse and the boys returned in a blink, looking no worse for wear. "It's all arranged," he said. "We'll have a bit of a job dispatching him into a waiting hackney carriage, but I've set the bait and I think he'll show up. Then it's down to the Isle of Dogs, where a chap will be waiting to take him in a little boat to a big boat and finally across the ocean."

Liv frowned. "I don't understand something. You must have worn the clothes you have on now. Didn't people question the way you looked?"

Morehouse laughed. "For the crowd we were dealing with, a gold coin answers all questions."

He pointed to Liv. "But you girls can come on the next round and do the honors with the box. We'll need a bit of finesse to trick Octavius. Wear some simple costumes if you like—long skirts you can just put over your jeans. We'll let the boys wait for us this time."

He grinned and gave Anthony a clap on the shoulder. "All for king and country, right?"

Morehouse's phone buzzed inside his sportcoat and he answered, listening for nearly a full minute before speaking. "Well, I still have them here with me," he said. "Get Tommy to drive—no one else."

He folded the phone and put it away. "I'm not sure what this is about, but its proximity to the time of our eavesdropping encounter at The Jellied Eel makes me suspect someone tattled to someone." He looked puzzled. "Pridgeon and McKnickel want to talk to me about you, and they don't mind if you hear it."

He led them away from Portobello Road to a deserted side street. "While we're waiting, girls, I'll outline tomorrow's plan. I've already counted on your cooperation. We'll all meet near Canary Wharf, right at the tube stop, and the boys will remain there. I'll travel with the pair of you to the Isle of Dogs, where we'll slip into seventeen-seventy-one early in the day and wait until dark.

"I've paid someone to deliver a message to Octavius Cumpston: that an anonymous gentleman needs a skilled negotiator to broker a deal, and he wants someone with Cumpston's skills to do the job. It involves the sale of two young slaves, for which he thinks he'll get a nice fee and possible referrals for future business."

He looked at Liv's hair. "You should get by, with your dark curls. I'll bring a wig for Frederica. Wear shawls over your heads to cover your necks and part of your faces. It'll be dark—long sleeves and long skirts should hide the rest well enough. Octavius's eyes will be on the fat profit he's expecting."

He raised his eyebrows. "In the best-case scenario, we'll show up, he'll show up and we'll dispatch him quickly. I've arranged for a carriage to meet us there." Morehouse stopped in front of a shop whose windows were filled to bursting with a jumble of used vases and figurines, appropriately named Bric-a-Brac, and waited, looking up and down the street.

"We'll tote him to the general area where we'll have left the boys in the present. The Docklands and Canary Wharf are bustling with activity in modern times, but back in the day, it was rather isolated—just right for our needs. There'll be only one business establishment about the place: a pub with no name. My, um, associates will be waiting there, and old Mr. Cumpston will be the one going on a journey, instead of his would-be victims. The three of us will disappear and rejoin the boys.

"Ah," he said, indicating a huge black car, "here are Pridgeon and McKnickel."

Chapter Thirty-five

A sleek, black limousine glided up to the curb and stopped. The driver looked scarier than Cumpston, with a purple birthmark on one cheek and a flattened nose. Through the dark glass, Liv could make out the shapes of two passengers in the last row of seats.

"Is it safe?" she asked.

"I know them," he replied, avoiding her question. "Get in. I'll introduce you." He opened the door of the cab and motioned for the four of them to enter. They sat cramped together, facing backward, behind the driver. Morehouse eased himself in beside the two men, who shifted to make room for him.

He began, "These are my unfortunate young friends."

"Yes, unfortunate," echoed one man. He wore a gray pinstripe suit and his shirt collar and cuffs were white, in contrast to the blue and white stripes of the shirt front. Heavy gold rings adorned his perfectly manicured fingers, and he pulled at his sleeve to reveal a Rolex watch on his left wrist. He glanced at it for a millisecond.

Liv suspected he already knew what time it was. He clasped

his hands and stared at the four of them, brown eyes unreadable in a carefully shaven, unsmiling face. She studied his companion. Not so well-groomed as his associate, this one had a worry line creasing his forehead in a deep groove. Sweat stained his unbuttoned shirt collar. A loosened necktie revealed a metal extender loop hanging from the top button. His gaze shifted nervously from the driver to the window, and back to the driver.

"Relax, McKnickel," ordered Morehouse. "Tommy works for all of us. We can count on him to take us around safely and keep the details to himself. And he can't hear through the glass anyway." He pointed to the roll-up window separating the front seat from the rest of the car.

Morehouse introduced the well-dressed man first. "This is Carmine Pridgeon, the brains of the firm, I like to say." He nodded toward his companion. "And this is Forrest McKnickel, the third associate."

McKnickel didn't appear to notice the slight. "It seems you've gone and created a problem that we now have to deal with," he vented. "You've gotten Cumpston on the warpath. I've never seen him like this. I really don't know what to do."

He chewed a fingernail and looked around, as if Cumpston might be listening. "Lancelot is the last person you want to get all stirred up and annoyed at you."

Morehouse smiled. "No. That last person would be me," he said slowly, unclasping his hands and crossing his arms. "But you're right to be worried about him. He's up to something."

McKnickel looked away from Morehouse and raised his hands in a helpless gesture. "If ever you could accuse anyone of simply being evil, it would be Cumpston." He shuddered and glanced at Pridgeon, who shook his head imperceptibly.

McKnickel ignored him and continued, "He—he does things for people, and then they're in his debt before they know it. He lets you know later what you owe him, and it's always much more than you feared. Fail to pay up and worse'll happen to you." Liv heard a little moan escape her throat. She covered her mouth. In her peripheral vision she caught a glimpse of Tommy, who seemed to be watching her thoughtfully.

McKnickel leaned forward, lowering his voice to a whisper. "Say someone owes you money. The chap may fall victim to a mugging. He won't report it—they never do."

"It's true," Pridgeon broke in, "Lancelot is a businessman, so if your victim wants revenge, he's happy to do a job for him as well. Try to do anything about it and you'll be looking over your shoulder the rest of your life. If you're still alive."

Morehouse sighed.   "That's the trouble with today's criminals—no sense of honor."

Pridgeon gave him a peculiar look and turned to Liv. "And now you've upset the balance of nature. Cumpston thinks someone is after him, and he's out for blood."

He shrugged and spread his hands. "Of course, he's often out for blood, but this is different. He's no longer detached. He's an extremely loose cannon, and I do not intend to be found in his line of fire. The question is: What do we do about it?"

He pointed a manicured finger at Morehouse. "It's mostly your fault," he accused. "There's something about you, beneath the charm. Cumpston fears, respects and despises you all at once. So if you've made a threat, you'd best carry it out."

He ignored the four young people, and murmured in Morehouse's ear, "What we can't absorb as assets, we dispose of as liabilities, if you get my meaning. Let us know very soon which one you are." He tapped on the glass behind Tommy and the door locks clicked open.

Afterward, they watched the car pull away and Frederica remarked, "They're vicious criminals, aren't they? I didn't expect them to look so. . .so ordinary."

Morehouse nodded. "They're people, trying to make their way in the world by thinking only of themselves. I've lived in three centuries now, and some things never change."

Liv thought he looked tired, and his face was more lined than she'd remembered.

"There'll be no point now trying to convince Lance we mean him no harm," he said. "He'll never believe it. But I'm a glass-is-half-full man, and the good news here is that Lancelot Cumpston is unlikely to cross our paths in the twenty-first century if he's Octavius's great-great-whatever-son, and that's one bit of history I won't regret tampering with."

Morehouse stood up straight and set his jaw. "There's much to do, and saving King George takes precedence for now."

Chapter Thirty-six

"It's a fine day for a kidnapping," said Morehouse, guiding the girls off a Docklands Light Railway car into the Island Gardens Station. They'd left the boys at Canary Wharf, with orders to keep an eye out for their return. "I'd completely given up this sort of thing, but who else could carry it off? Ironically, Octavius is perfect for the job, but he'll be unavailable." Morehouse laughed at his own joke.

Liv and Frederica made their way to the restroom, where they slipped long skirts over their jeans. The box was wrapped in a shawl. Morehouse was waiting for them, and they made their way outside.

It wasn't a long walk to the Isle of Dogs, and no one paid much attention to two eccentrically dressed girls. Morehouse had come out of the men's room dressed like a beggar and he walked alongside them now, practicing a variety of limps and applying streaks of soot to his face. He ruffled his hair and smiled at a pair of middle-aged ladies, who jaywalked to get to the other side of the street.

"We'll have a pleasant wait," he told the girls. "We can sit on the bank of the Thames, out of the way, and watch people take the ferry over to Greenwich."

He reached into the deep pockets of the loose, ragged jacket he wore over his sportcoat and pulled out bananas, cheese crackers, bottles of water and paper napkins. "I even brought supper. All we need now is for the sun to set."

Liv loosened the shawl, linked arms with Frederica and Morehouse, and adjusted the drawers of the box.

It came out of the dark through the mist, its wheels on the cobblestones barely audible over the clip-clopping of a single horse's hooves. A dingy yellow lantern made a feeble attempt to cut through the fog, but it was like trying to shine a light through pudding.

Morehouse motioned the girls off the street and onto the curb as the hackney carriage came into view. The carriage's two wheels were almost as high as the horse's rear flanks, but the cab was small. Even with the driver outside, behind the cab, Liv wondered how the four of them would squeeze in.

Morehouse had instructed them to stand on the sidewalk and wait for Octavius. Morehouse would take it from there.

Liv fingered the box nervously under her shawl, feeling the hinges beneath its thin material. If something went wrong and Morehouse couldn't protect them, could she get both herself and Frederica safely back? As soon as she thought of it, she realized it didn't matter. They wouldn't desert him. . .even though he'd probably scream at them to do just that.

Heavy footsteps sounded in the lane, and a thick, cloaked figure approached. The man stopped within an arm's reach. Liv and Frederica looked down meekly, as they'd been told to do. Liv's heart thudded in her chest. If he looked too carefully, he'd realize they weren't Africans. And while she knew he couldn't recognize them from the fateful night in the Octagon Room that hadn't happened yet, it was unnerving to be this close to King George's assassin.

"So, it's like that, is it?" His mouth curled downward at the sight of the girls. "You're just thrown out in the street! I suppose

I'm expected to pay your cab fare—an expense I shall have to pass on."

He blew out a snort and peered into the blackness beyond the carriage. "Now then, where's your, er, sponsor?"

Morehouse stepped out of the dark and grabbed him from behind. "Been looking for me, Cumpston? It appears you found me."

"Take your filthy hands off—" He twisted his neck to get a look at Morehouse and gasped, eyes bulging. "You!"

Cumpston did a visual sweep: first the girls, then the carriage, and finally down to the tip of the blade glinting in the feeble light as it pricked his silk shirt front. Sweat trickled down his forehead as he appeared to put the puzzle together in his mind.

"You don't want to know what I've done with this dagger, do you now?" Morehouse said.

Cumpston's fingers touched his parted lips and he squeaked, "Where are you taking me?"

"Oh, you're going on a nice Caribbean holiday. Well, not technically the Caribbean—more like the Western Atlantic. A lovely spot on Barbados. If you fancy turtle meat and working for a living, you'll have a grand time. There's a family at the old Beringer plantation who can always use an extra field hand."

"A slave? You're going to sell me as a slave? That's illegal— it's kidnapping!" Cumpston's voice cracked and Liv came close to feeling sorry for him.

"Hah!" Morehouse scoffed. "As if you weren't just trying to do the same thing yourself." He wagged a finger at Cumpston.

"But let me put your mind at ease. Though hardly anyone takes on indentured servants anymore, that's what you'll be— not a slave. Why, in seven short years, you can start saving up money to come back home. Think how fit and lean you'll be!" He pushed an index finger into Cumpston's ample belly, and it disappeared up to the last knuckle. "The rural east coast of Barbados is picturesque, with places like Cattlewash and Ragged Point." Cumpston cringed and wrung his hands.

"Of course, there's always an alternative." Morehouse flashed his trademark smile—the one that melted women's hearts and struck fear in his enemies.

"Ooh, an alternative. Yes—anything, anything at all." Cumpston pointed to his pocket. "I'll pay—I have money, you know. I have influence." He waited, quivering and breathing shallowly.

The pirate's eyes turned to blue steel. The girls shivered as he whispered into Cumpston's ear, just loudly enough for them to hear. "The alternative is that I slit your sorry throat right here. After all, that would be better than reporting to His Majesty that while you can't even catch an old pirate for him, you were plotting to kill both the king and his prizewinning clockmaker."

"But I never!" spluttered Cumpston.

"Oh, he'll think you did," replied Morehouse. "And by the time I get through making the case against you, he'll be falling over himself to pardon me—maybe even reward me."

He pulled a length of rope from each sleeve and tied Cumpston's hands in front of him with one piece. He tackled Cumpston's thrashing legs and threw the other rope to the girls. "Here—get the other rope round his ankles. And be sure the knot is fast."

Frederica took it gingerly and held it out to Liv.

Morehouse laughed. "What's wrong, ladies? Don't like to get your hands dirty? Do it, and be quick about it!"

Liv swallowed hard and took the rope, tying it the best she could. She glanced at the cab driver a few times, but he made a show of not watching any of their goings-on. Frederica moved off the curb and walked around in front of Morehouse and his quarry, ready for further instructions. Morehouse nodded his approval. "Liv," he said, not dropping his gaze from Cumpston, whom he still held down, "crawl around and reach into the left front pocket of my coat. Pull out the piece of rope that's in there —that's right—now the two of you—No!"

Liv's head had come within Cumpston's reach, and his pudgy fingers grabbed her hair and pulled her off-balance. She winced as the cobblestones scraped skin from an elbow and the palm she planted on the bricks to steady herself. Cumpston proved surprisingly strong, not letting go of the handful of curly hair in his grasp.

Suddenly, she was set free. How Morehouse had done it she couldn't tell, but he yawned and shook his head at Cumpston.

"I'd demand an apology, but I'm not convinced it would be sincere. Instead, I'll give you a demerit." He slapped Cumpston's face with an open hand, the sound echoing against the bricks of the narrow street and close-in buildings. Liv bit her lip. Her carelessness had caused Cumpston pain and she didn't like it, even if her scalp and skin were still throbbing.

Morehouse used the third rope to wrap around Cumpston's torso, trussing him up with his arms at his sides. He spoke in a casual tone as he worked.

"There's a schooner moored in the harbor that's been there for several weeks. They're just waiting to fill up so they can push off for Barbados. You'll like the mix of interesting people you'll meet working in the sugar fields, Cumpston: Irish Catholics, gypsies, captured natives, in addition to the Africans."

He cocked his head toward the cab door and Liv ran to open it, while the cab driver climbed down without comment and helped pick up Cumpston.

"In fact, I'm tempted to wager you'll start making contacts while you're still chained to your bunk in the ship. By the time you've been in Barbados for a year, you'll have your own network and a whole new life for yourself. You may grow fond of the Bajan way of life and not even want to come back to England. Isn't that right?"

Cumpston gave Morehouse a look of pure evil. "I hope you hang for this, you filthy pirate. I hope they hang you and then skewer your head on a stake in the harbor for the gulls to peck your eyes out." He glared at Liv and Frederica. "And that goes for these shameless brats, too."

Morehouse nodded at the girls. "If we're through with the niceties, let's all climb in, shall we? We'll escort our guest to the gateway of his new life."

Chapter Thirty-seven

"Our problem with Lance may be solved, if that's his ancestor we relocated." Morehouse's voice sounded upbeat, and Liv dared to hope he was right.

They'd returned to the present and were retracing their steps, headed back to Island Gardens Station to catch the train. Frederica pulled off her wig and handed it to Morehouse. He put it under his jacket and said, "Finish in the restrooms. Two minute limit. The clock is ticking in real time now."

The journey back to Canary Wharf Station was blessedly dull. The hard part was over, and Liv was glad to be sitting. She'd been surprised to find the relief made her legs shaky. Mudchute Station, Crossharbour, Heron Quay—she could relax a little and enjoy the quaint names as they passed.

"I'll just stop at a pay telephone and check my voice mail," Morehouse told them as they exited the train. "Didn't want to take the mobile with me and lose it in a scuffle. That would have planted a very disturbing object in the past."

He pulled coins from his pocket and counted them. "If we're lucky, a nervous message I received from McKnickel this morning will no longer be in my mailbox. He was demanding I come up with an idea today for dealing with Lance. Tee-hee—if he only knew!" He took long strides to a telephone on a wall and fed it coins. The girls trotted over to join him.

"Look," whispered Frederica to Liv, "I see the guys!" Cal and Anthony were sitting on a bench just outside, eating ice cream and looking around.

Morehouse pushed buttons and held the receiver to his ear, frowning. Too much time was passing for everything to be okay, and Liv tapped Frederica and pointed to the pirate, who pressed his finger to disconnect and made another call.

"It's me...Yeah, I got McKnickel's message. . .I did try something—not sure why it didn't work. I think it's not safe hanging about—send Tommy with the car, will you?. . .At Canary Wharf. Pick us up in fifteen minutes."

He replaced the receiver. "Let's collect the boys and get out of here."

Liv and Frederica followed. Outside, Cal and Anthony leaped off their bench and met them halfway. "Well?" asked Anthony.

"Minor inconvenience," replied Morehouse, as the boys fell in step. "Tommy's picking us up. I'm sure Octavius had an interesting time of it in Barbados, but somehow Lance is still here—can you believe it? Mean as ever. Pridgeon says he's on the warpath, and a couple of his goons spotted us when we first arrived. They've probably been keeping an eye on you two – don't know if they saw the girls and me get on the Light Rail. We'll keep our pace moderate, avoid attracting attention, and walk to the nearest underground station. We'll enter as if we're going to take the tube, then double back and wait for the car."

He looked directly at Liv. "From there, I'm having Tommy take us to the nearest police station to drop off the four of you, where you're to call your parents. Tell the police what you know about Lance, which isn't much. It'll give them something to go on while I get with Pridgeon and try to work on damage control."

He rubbed his face. "McKnickel I'm not sure about, but that's not your concern. And you'd best start coming up with a believable story about what the three of us were doing at the Isle of Dogs. That's not going to be easy."

"I hate lying to my parents!" Liv balled up a fist and hit her other hand.

"Can't be helped," said Morehouse, no trace of sympathy in his voice.

Chapter Thirty-eight

They made their way to the Underground. Unlike its Light Rail namesake, the Canary Wharf tube station beckoned them from the street with a glass canopy that became a transparent cathedral when they entered the escalator area.

"Can we turn around yet?" Anthony asked Morehouse.

"In a minute. Move forward about five more yards, then circle back to your—"

Liv was closest to him, and he pulled her back. "Uh-oh."

He turned on his heel and walked back toward the entrance, his mouth set in a tight line. The others followed, saying nothing.

Liv risked a look backward. Everyone seemed to be going about their own business, but two men, standing still and talking to each other, seemed out of place.

They were dressed in suits, but neither was carrying a briefcase. The slicked-back hair of one and the earring of the other clashed with the image of business types Liv had seen on the streets and up close on the tube trains.

As she watched, Slick pulled a mobile from inside his jacket and pushed a button, his acne-scarred complexion highlighted in the afternoon sun streaming through the roof. While he talked earnestly, Earring cocked his head in another direction and began walking purposefully toward the exit, ahead of them. Slick glanced over at their group and continued talking. Liv quickly turned away.

Morehouse whispered in her ear as they hurried toward the escalator, "It appears Nigel's going to watch us, probably keep Lance informed or call for reinforcements. I'd say Eddie's gone to get their car. We can't wait around for Tommy."

Down, down they rode. Signs informed them they were about to board the Jubilee Line. Morehouse bought tickets and led them through the stiles onto a waiting train. "What are we going to do?" asked Liv.

"Lose those buggers, for starters. Then get all of us to a police station. There's West End Central, or Marylebone, both accessible on the Central Line."

Morehouse steepled his fingers. "But first, some evasive maneuvers. We'll transfer at London Bridge and ride to Camden Town, hop off and come back in the opposite direction on a different loop—"

"I get it!" Anthony broke in, pointing at the route map on the wall above the seats. "It's the Northern Line." He traced his fingers in the air. "We go past Old Street and Angel, then back by Euston, Warren Street and Tottenham Court Road. We switch right there to the Central Line."

"Sheesh!" said Liv. "I'd ask you to repeat that, but I'm afraid you might be able to."

"No need to be sarcastic," Anthony replied. "I've just never met a map I didn't love."

The shift from Jubilee to Northern was uneventful, and the next transfer promised more of the same—not a bad guy in sight. They waited on the platform at Tottenham Court Road, ready to board for Oxford Circus with the midafternoon crowd.

Liv could almost remember how it felt to be normal. The arriving train slowed to a stop and disembarking passengers surged from the train cars, indifferent to those eager to take their places.

Except for one.   Liv's heart nearly stopped.

Lance Cumpston emerged, looking straight at them.   "He's not even trying to hide.   It's like he wants us to see him," she whispered.

Morehouse didn't seem to believe his eyes.   "He shouldn't be here.   How could he possibly have known where we are?   I'm sure we lost Nigel and Eddie a good while back."

Cal offered, "Maybe he has more helpers than we thought."

"A chilling possibility," replied Morehouse, leading them away from the train until enough people came between them and Cumpston.   Then he inclined his head toward the train and steered them back in.

Cal shuddered.   "It's like we have a homing beacon on us."

They held their breath, hoping he would think they'd made their way up to the street.   Cumpston followed the crowd, scanning it like a lion looking for just the right zebra, while the new wave of travelers boarded.

"We'll go a few more stops, then get off and find a way to call the police."

Frederica said, "Something's made him look back.   Here he comes.   He's getting on again—in the car behind us!"

Chapter Thirty-nine

"Off—now!" Morehouse gave Cal a shove forward and grabbed both Liv and Frederica by an arm, nearly lifting them off their feet as he raced out the door on Cal's heels.

Anthony followed as closely as he dared without tripping Cal, and barely made it to the platform as the doors shut on the tail of his windbreaker.

In a flash, Morehouse was in front of him, ripping open the Velcro fastenings of the jacket and grabbing Anthony around the waist.

Liv held her breath as she watched her brother's arms jerk backward, pulled by the train's forward motion. The screams of a woman passenger caused her to look up.

Right in front of them, playing the hero, was Lance Cumpston, straining at the doors, struggling to pry them apart. Other passengers in the car shouted, cheering him on, and two men leaped up from their seats to help him.

Their efforts failed to open the heavy doors, but it didn't matter. Morehouse pulled Anthony free from the sleeves, turning them inside out, and the train surged ahead with the jacket blowing crazily alongside like a tortured windsock.

"Let's get out of here," Morehouse said, not wasting a second as he made his way toward the exit. "To the other side."

They crossed the common space and slipped through the entry to the opposite platform. "Lance is probably going to get off at the next stop—Oxford Circus. I hope he'll think we've gone above ground and kept moving. We'll wait here and take the next train going in the opposite direction, then get off at Holborn or switch to the Piccadilly Line. Somewhere I hope there's a bobby who'll listen."

Liv made no effort to hide the worry in her voice. "The things you know about Lance Cumpston could get you killed— could get any of us killed."

"I'll think of something." Morehouse looked up at the schedule sign. The LED readout promised the next train would arrive in ten minutes. "That's a long time," he said, frowning.

Two minutes dragged by, and the five of them waited without speaking. Liv crossed her fingers and hoped Morehouse was busy coming up with a plan.

She looked around and wished there were people around. She would have felt safer in a crowd. Surely passengers would begin to arrive soon.

Footsteps clattered down the hallway outside the platform area. Liv peeked around a snack machine into the open space, and relief washed over her. It was Tommy, talking earnestly on a mobile and looking in all directions.

She glanced back at Morehouse, who couldn't see Tommy from his seat on the bench. Morehouse didn't have a mobile with him. The double-crossing driver was probably giving Lance's people a blow-by-blow account of his search.

She raced back. "It's Tommy," she whispered, shaking her head and making a thumbs-down sign.

"Hide," he said. "I'll deal with him." He set off at a run, leaving the four of them standing, while Tommy's footsteps came louder and faster.

Frederica pulled them to the edge of the platform and pointed to the tracks. "Down there!"

"But the train's coming in five minutes now!" said Liv.

"So we'll stay there for four-and-a-half. Maybe it'll give Morehouse time to get Tommy out of here."

"Come on, Cal," whispered Anthony, shoving his friend toward the edge of the concrete.

"We can't leave him on his own!" Cal dug in his heels and tried to resist, but the other dragged him along.

Frederica went first, jumping and landing with surprising lightness, just reaching down to the rail to steady herself. Her hands came up black from the soot and soiled Cal's shirt as she caught him to keep him from sitting straight down between the tracks.

Liv leaned down to go next, then recoiled at the sight of a dozen or more black objects, scurrying away from them. "Rats!" she breathed.

"Mice." Anthony's mouth was in her ear as he pushed her off the platform and scrambled after her.

Frederica and Cal managed to catch Liv and keep her from hitting the rail, but Anthony landed with a thwack and a groan.

"Are you okay?" Liv asked guiltily. "I'm sorry—it's just that rats are so nasty, not to mention big and black and scary."

"I told you they were mice, and yeah, I guess I'm okay." He rose to a crouch and huddled with the others. "And for your information, they're actually brown. They just look black because they're covered with coal dust. Kind of like me."

"How could you possibly know about mice in the Underground?"

"I looked it up."

"Did not."

"Did so."

"Shut up!" said Cal and Frederica together, as the sound of footsteps approached again.

"Anthony? Cal? Where'd you go?" Morehouse peered over the edge of the platform. "What are you doing down there? Don't you know there's a train coming?"

He leaned down, gave a hand to Liv and pulled her out, then let her help Frederica while he got the boys up. "Tommy didn't see me. Let's take the next train. Dust yourselves off—there'll be a crowd in here any minute."

They sat in facing seats, except for Morehouse. He stood, a few feet away from them, holding onto a pole and discreetly examining the ends of the car. Liv knew what he was looking for: Cumpston's thugs on neighboring cars. They'd escaped once. She wasn't sure they could do it again.

She turned and studied Frederica, sitting next to her and looking out the window as if she did this sort of thing every day. She seemed to be functioning as well as the rest of them right now. If you didn't know she was a cutter, you might not ever guess.

Liv could see how cutting could be a hidden epidemic. The victims didn't seem to talk about it, and it was easy for everyone else to ignore. Bringing it up was difficult—for the cutter, and for friends and family.

Liv brushed her blackened jeans with blackened hands. What would a real friend do? She'd think about it later.

The train slowed for Holborn, and Morehouse came toward them, nodding. They followed him and fell in step with the crowd. "We'll try for Kingsway," he said. "It's a big street—lots of places to lose someone who's trying to tail you."

Chapter Forty

They slowed to a walk on High Holborn, trying to blend into the crowd.

"Blast," said Morehouse. "Don't look, but Lance is right across the street. Nigel and Eddie won't be far behind."

He pointed to a nearby side street. "Run a few blocks, then turn right onto any street. That'll send you toward Kingsway, a major thoroughfare. Find the police—any way you can. Stop someone on the sidewalk—ask them to call nine-nine-nine on their mobile phone. Or dash into a store and make some noise. Whatever it takes. I'll go after Lance."

Anthony grabbed Morehouse's arm with both of his and held on. "What do you mean, go after him? He's coming at you! And I bet he has a gun! You don't. . .do you?"

Morehouse pulled Anthony away with his free arm and smiled. "Perhaps not, but Lance doesn't know that. Remember who I am, Anthony—who I really am." He took Liv's hand and placed it on Anthony's arm, giving her a meaningful look while his voice remained casual. "I've been in worse situations and done all right for myself."

She took the hint and was on the move before he spoke again. "Get out of here—fast." He gave Cal and Frederica a shove. "And don't look back."

They zigzagged for a couple of blocks, then spotted Slick – who must be Nigel—on a side street. Unfortunately, he spotted them, too, and nearly lost his footing spinning around to come after them.

"Could be worse," said Frederica as they jogged, staying well ahead of him, for the moment. "At least he's not pulling out his mobile. He must be alone."

"Don't count on it," said Liv. "Do you know where we are?"

"I'm guessing if we turn up the next side street, we might end up on Kingsway in a block or two. But we're no longer close to High Holborn." She panted and pointed in the opposite direction. "If we go that way, there's a small park—Lincoln's Inn Fields—and a little museum in an old house. It might be a good place to hide, but I think we'd best head toward the main street and hope to avoid Nigel."

They came to an alley, and Liv dared to hope they'd lost their pursuers. Then an arm reached out and clotheslined Cal. His feet flew out from under him, and in the second before he hit the cobblestones, Eddie grabbed Frederica from behind and twisted her arm hard enough to make her cry out. Nigel closed in, but Liv and Anthony tackled him, while Frederica kicked backward like a mule at Eddie, hitting the bottom of a kneecap.

She left him hopping on his other leg, howling with pain, and the four of them shoved Nigel facedown on the pavers, knocking him unconscious. It would buy them a few minutes.

If only they knew the back streets even a little, Liv lamented. But a couple of dead ends cost them precious time and led them to an area with little traffic.

Eddie, limping and decidedly unhappy, came around a corner. Nigel, apparently impervious to head blows, caught up with him.

"They're coming—straight from the way we want to go!" Cal's voice was high-pitched with anxiety.

Anthony asked, "What now?"

Liv rolled her eyes. "Run the other way—what else?"

"Come on," Frederica said, sprinting across the street ahead of them and up the sidewalk for a block-and-a-half, then onto the stairs of a tall townhouse.

Maybe it was the home of someone she knew, someone with unusual taste. They must be rich—the place was huge. Its front stuck out farther than those of its neighbors. The full-sized stone maidens near the roof were eye-catching, if strange. On the front porch, in front of two full-length windows, two iron boot scrapers were mounted, though no one was likely to accumulate mud in a city of solidly paved streets and sidewalks.

They all trotted behind Frederica, whom Liv assumed would ring the bell or pound on the door. Instead, she simply turned the knob and opened the door, motioning for the others to hurry inside. "It's a museum," she whispered between gasps, as they entered a large foyer paneled in dark wood. "No one at the desk—must be a slow day."

Liv looked at the donation box and read the plaque: "Sir John Soane's House." Where had she heard that before? Anthony's laptop. He'd been showing the Web site to Cal one day at home, what seemed like a lifetime ago.

She turned to Anthony, whose eyes widened as he realized the same thing. "Well, you wanted to visit."

He said, "I remember the basic layout from the Internet. This floor is all on the tour. The tomb of Seti is close to here, and downstairs is where the old guy would sit in the dark with his creepy artifacts. Right over our heads you can go all the way up to an attic loft with a balcony. Good place to hide and watch what's going on."

Frederica offered, "I know my way around pretty well, too, thanks to yet another school field trip. I think downstairs is best—I seem to remember there's some sort of exit there."

Frederica led the way and Liv followed, assuming the boys were right behind them. Halfway down, she heard rapid footsteps too far away to be Cal and Anthony. She looked back. The boys were gone.

She tried to reverse directions, but Frederica pulled her back.

She struggled to break free. "They may have grabbed them!"

"And they may not have," whispered Frederica, pulling Liv along. "And if they have, we must get out of here and call the police. We can't do this alone."

Reluctantly, Liv followed, and they looked around for an exit, then froze at the sound of staccato footsteps on the stairs—too loud to be made by the boys' tennis shoes and too fast to be a tourist.

"Go!" hissed Frederica, but Liv was already in motion. They made their way through a series of twist-and-turn passages, stopping in front of an interior door labeled "China Closet." The heavy footsteps pounded on the stone floor, slowing down as they came closer. Then there was quiet, even more chilling than the noise had been.

Liv tried the closet's doorknob and to her surprise, it opened. She glanced at Frederica, who nodded, and in they went.

"We're not safe here," whispered Liv. "I'm pulling out the box." She reached into her skirt and shawl bundle. "I can't see— I'll have to do it by feel. I'm just going to pull out the ones' drawer a little. It should take us back a year or two."

"That's good. Everything will be the same. We'll walk upstairs, step behind something, and come back to the present. Surely we can find the boys and some staff to help us."

"Great plan. Hope you remember the way out of here."

The shadows of feet appeared in the crack of light under the door, and Frederica quietly took hold of the doorknob. She pulled hard, grunting with the effort, but the knob turned and the door opened a quarter-inch.

Liv fumbled with the box, leaned her head against Frederica to make sure they had contact, and clawed at the drawers.

Chapter Forty-one

The doorknob stopped turning, and everything was quiet. "Do you think we're locked in?" Liv breathed into Frederica's ear.

"Let's find out." She turned the knob and pushed gently. The door opened and Frederica peeked into the hall. "I don't see anyone."

Linking arms and tiptoeing from the closet, they stepped into dim light, though it was mid-afternoon. They crept along the hallway, inching back toward the stairs.

Liv held the drawers of the box in position and showed them to Frederica—eighteen thirty-five. Frederica nodded and made a thumbs-up sign, then froze as a thin, reedy voice floated toward them from behind. The words were slow and deliberate, as if the speaker were writing as he talked to himself.

"Thursday, eighteenth June, eighteen hundred and thirty-five. Dined alone." There was a pause, followed by a sigh and a wheeze. "Again."

They went a yard farther, silent as the ghosts Liv could imagine might inhabit this place. If they could make their way up the stairs and past any hired help, they should be able to get outside, travel back to the present, and scream for help.

"You may as well step in here where I can see you." The voice was stronger now, and Liv marveled that the man had been able to hear them.

"If you're a robber, you can knock me in the head whilst you're about it, and finish me off. I miss my late wife, and I won't mind joining her."

The girls looked at each other, shrugged, and walked toward the voice.

An old man sat in a chair, holding a quill pen and an open book. A short candle, fixed to a human skull, provided the only light. Wax had dripped and built up on the skull, giving it an odd little hat. Sir John Soane stated the obvious. "I was writing in my journal."

Frederica stepped forward. "We're sorry to have disturbed you, Sir John, and we mean you no harm. We came here, well, sort of by accident, and we don't intend to stay."

The old man's skin appeared almost transparent in the dim light, and his face bore an unsettling resemblance to the skull candleholder. "I've been a collector of oddities and a student of secrets for a long time now, and I think I know how you came to be in my house."

Liv stammered, "Uh, we just wandered in. The door was unlocked."

Soane chuckled. "My dear children, I'm far too old and tired for games. I particularly enjoy the legends that surround things I collect, or would like to collect.

"There's an intriguing story of a golden disk, cast by an ancient South American tribe. It enabled the makers to travel through time.

"In their wisdom, they knew it was too dangerous a thing to use much, so the secret was closely guarded. Only one elder at a time knew how to make a device to activate the disk."

He leaned forward in his chair. "Hah! There's my confirmation I see it in your eyes. I'd hoped the Quimbaya legend was true. I don't suppose you'd want to sell it, would you?"

"Oh, no sir, we couldn't," replied Liv.

"I thought not."

Curiosity got the better of her. "Even if you knew the legend, how could you be so sure we'd time traveled?"

He wagged a finger at them and grinned. "It wasn't as much of a leap of logic as you might think. In fact, it was beautifully simple. You weren't here, and then you were. Your accents are strange, your clothing is strange, and you're. . ."—he poked the air with a finger, searching for the right word—". . .cheeky."

His expression sobered. "I have only two concerns. First, are you using this extraordinary gift in a frivolous fashion, or out of necessity?" He peered at them over the pince-nez spectacles perched on his long nose.

"We were running for our lives," said Liv, "and trying to save three others."

Soane nodded. "That, at least, is the truth. I hear it in your voice. Second—and it's a self-centered question from a bitter old man—what about my work? All my beautiful buildings, and this house?" He waved his hand. "I poured my heart and soul into it all, and look at me. Feeble and lonely, hoping someone remembers me. Does anyone?"

Frederica moved a step closer. "Sir John, I'll just tell you the truth, because I don't think you'd respect anything less. There's not much left of your public buildings, but you're still regarded as a great architect."

She raised her head toward the ceiling. "And this place is known all over the world. It's been visited and loved and cared for by generations of people who appreciate what you did."

"Well, now, that cheers a fellow up, doesn't it? An ancient mystery solved, and good news about the future. I'm doubly glad you came."

He pointed to the hallway. "The housekeeper has taken off early, so you may go anywhere you wish and travel back to your own time. There's no one else in the house. For some reason, I can't seem to keep live-in help anymore. No one wants to spend the night here. Pity—the house is wonderfully spooky at night."

Sir John dipped his quill in a nearby inkpot and began to write again. "Spoke with time travelers after dinner. It seems the legend of Quimbaya is true."

He closed the book, picked up the skull, and gave a start when he saw the girls still standing there. "Oh, I thought we'd said good bye. Thank you for an interesting evening, but you'd best be going. Good luck to you."

"Thanks," they said in unison.

They hurried along the hallway. "Let's walk to the gift shop area," said Liv. "When we go back, maybe there's a phone at the cash register."

"Right. Once we've traveled, you look for the boys. I'll make the call and join you."

Chapter Forty-two

The quiet of eighteen thirty-five was shattered by the chaos of the present. Staff and visitors had gathered near the stairs, yelling and pointing up to the loft area. Mobiles were everywhere, and two people were using theirs to take video of something happening above.

Liv looked up and saw Anthony, struggling with Nigel, trying to keep from being pushed over the railing. Cal was tugging at Eddie with one arm and pounding him with the other in an attempt to keep him from helping Nigel. If Anthony fell, it would be a multistory drop onto the stone floor.

She screamed, "No-ooo!" and ran toward the stairs. Shouts and footsteps came from behind her, and she was knocked aside. She heard the thud of her head hitting the iron railing, and everything went black.

When she opened her eyes, it surprised her to see that the floor had zoomed up to just below her shoulders. The walls and ceiling spun around merrily at first, then slowed as a pair of arms lifted her head and shoulders. She looked up.

It was Tommy. She tried to struggle and fell back, watching bright spots dance around his face. As they disappeared, she could make out more shapes. Frederica, Anthony and Cal.

None of them seemed worried about Tommy. She needed to save them all, but she felt so tired. She'd just close her eyes for a minute and save them after she'd had a little rest. . .

Bursts of static and unintelligible talk woke her, and she watched Tommy pull a walkie-talkie from inside his jacket. "This is Harper. Yeah, the kids are safe, but we need an ambulance for one of them."

He looked down at Liv, but before he could speak, the yellow-green jacket of a police officer came into blurry view. The woman reached down and touched Tommy on the shoulder. "Sir, we have two mobile units and several officers on foot trailing Cumpston. The bug in his suit jacket is still working. We've been able to hear everything, even his mobile conversations. He's chasing Morehouse."

"Right. Let's go the extra mile to save Morehouse if we can. It's Cumpston and his goons we're after."

He turned to Liv. "Not the best timing, was it? You lot being pursued by Cumpston and friends just as we were closing in. Wish we'd been a day earlier."

He grinned and pointed his thumb behind him. "But it worked out all right for your brother, didn't it? My boys dashing up the stairs—a bit fast, but I hope you'll forgive them for knocking you down on their way to save him."

He pulled Liv up to a sitting position and motioned to the boys and Frederica. "Here, take care of her. And don't let her go to sleep."

The policewoman held up a hand for silence, and everyone listened to Cumpston's voice, relayed through her walkie.

"He's headed to the Silver Vaults. It looks like. . .yeah, he's going in."

"We're on it," replied a second voice. "Right behind you. The Silver Vaults, eh? There won't be an easy way for him to get away from us."

They could hear Cumpston's labored breathing and he

gasped, "That could get dangerous in a hurry."

The second voice drawled, "Yeah, but it could also be a bit of fun."

"Stop it. And be there by the time I get there."

Cumpston's phone beeped as he disconnected the call, and the room was filled with the amplified sound of his shoes hitting the sidewalk, closing in on Morehouse. Tommy said to the policewoman, "My team's out of here. Truss Nigel and Eddie up like chickens and treat them as very dangerous. We'll charge 'em with attempted murder of a child." He spoke into his walkie. "I'm on my way. I want a couple of extra squad cars and an ambulance at the Vaults."

He waved to Liv and the others. "Wish us luck."

Chapter Forty-three

Morehouse wondered which would get him first—the burning in his lungs or the screaming of overtaxed leg muscles. A few years of the soft life, and he was out of shape. But even in his pirate prime, he'd've been no match for these pursuers. With their mobile phones and cars, they could run him to ground without exerting themselves.

The sidewalks of Chancery Lane, in London's historic legal district, offered no cover, and the next tube station was probably a three-minute run. Too risky.

He jogged past the entrance to the Silver Vaults, where he'd done business a few times in the sprawling underground-safe-turned-mall.   Room-sized shops sold everything from old coins to fine jewelry, used teaspoons to precious silver antiques.

There were plenty of nooks and crannies for him to hide in, but they could fast become places to get cornered, and the way in was probably also the only way out. He tried not to think about that as he went in.

Passing several little shops, slowing his pace, he willed his heart rate to slow down and wondered what to do next.

At a jewelry shop window, he pretended to examine the selection of vintage watches while checking the glass for reflections of Lance or his boys. Satisfied, he moved on, matching his step to the meandering stroll of the few customers in the long hall.

With Lance nowhere to be seen, Morehouse entered a shop, empty except for an elderly merchant seated on a stool by the cash register. Browsing at a table near the window, he stood perfectly still. Something—some heightened awareness told him danger was coming.

Sure enough, two strangers came into view. Their senses must have been as hyped-up as his—one of them scanned the shops and his eyes locked on Morehouse. Without a word, he placed a hand on his buddy's arm.

Morehouse's mind raced. Who were these two? Where were Nigel and Eddie? If they weren't here, they must have gone after the kids. He had to get out and find them.

A sword at the back of the shop caught his eye. He darted past the surprised shopkeeper and pulled it off the wall.

"Are you interested in that piece, sir? No silver on it, but it's a very fine seventeenth-century hunting hanger. The blade is single-edged and curved, as you can see. Staghorn handle's in perfect condition, and the owner's name's engraved on the knucklebar."

"Hmm. . .R. Clark. Didn't know him, but it was before my time."

The owner gave him a puzzled look.

"Could be a naval officer's sword," said Morehouse, hefting the weapon and keeping an eye on the shop windows at the same time.

"Very good, sir! Naval officers in the sixteen hundreds often used hunting hangers. This one's priced at seven hundred fifty pounds, but I could let it go for seven hundred."

Lance's minions slipped in at the shop door.

"You wouldn't happen to have a shield about the place, would you?" Morehouse grabbed the handle of a silver tea service, sending the teapot, sugar bowl and creamer clattering to the floor, pulling the tray to his chest for protection.

The dealer's mouth popped open, but he made only a squeak, as a strong arm reached from behind and gripped his neck like a vise. Lance's helper held a gun to the old man's head with his free hand, while his partner rushed at Morehouse.

The partner pulled his own gun from a shoulder holster and aimed it at Morehouse as he closed the distance between them.

Morehouse feinted to his attacker's left, thrusting the sword just enough to distract him, then lunged and flicked the gun from the man's hand. He'd meant only to knock it to the floor, but the tip of the blade nicked the webbing between the thug's forefinger and thumb, and a small red fountain spurted.

"Shoot him, would you?" he shouted, waving his hand at his partner. "Look—I'm bleeding, and that blade's probably filthy with germs. I'll need a tetanus sho—"

A metallic thunk interrupted his request and he sank to the floor, unconscious.

"You shouldn't've gone and done that!" the first thug shouted at Morehouse, pressing his gun barrel hard at the merchant's right temple. "I can hang onto the old man whilst shooting you, and still have my hostage."

It was true. The hostage was a couple of inches shorter, several pounds lighter, and a few decades older than his captor. And his right arm was jammed up against his body. His left hand was free, which probably counted for nothing.

Still, bravado had saved him before. He grinned and said, "You don't want to fire that thing in here. The bullet might ricochet right off this tray and fly back at you."

The shopkeeper's left arm snaked backward. His fingers closed around a tall silver candlestick on a nearby table. Slowly, silently, the candlestick rose.

"Sorry, chum, a bit of silver's no match for a bul—"

The merchant nodded in satisfaction as Morehouse whistled and said, "These lads have trouble finishing their sentences, don't they? How'd you manage that?"

"I snatched the nearest piece of inventory I could reach. I still play tennis. . ." He smiled. "And I'm left-handed."

Just Lance now to deal with, and he might get out of here

yet. Morehouse shouted, "Call the police!" and waved the sword. "Need to borrow this a bit longer."

The dealer looked up in dismay. "There's more?"

He held the door for Morehouse, turning the "Open" sign to "Closed." He followed him out, slamming the door shut and twisting the key in the deadbolt lock while he struggled to pull his mobile out of his pocket.

Chapter Forty-four

Morehouse took off at a dead run, vowing to join a gym if he lived through this. He hadn't gone far before Lance's men had found him, but that point of geography might play in his favor now, as the main entrance was only about fifty yards away.

All the commotion had drawn a small crowd out into the mall area, and mobile phones appeared at ears, with variations of, "There's a lunatic running through the Vaults with a sword!" pinged off the walls and down the hallways. It occurred to him that the average bystander might assume he was the criminal, and he hoped to be able to sort that out later.

Another ten yards or so. Then what?

There was no time to consider it. Out the door of the last shop came Lance, his gun pointed straight at Morehouse. Screams split the air and people scattered.

Lance seemed oblivious to the sounds. He was completely focused, holding his gun with both hands and glowering at Morehouse.

Morehouse knew that look—he'd seen it in Octavius's eyes not long ago. Ironic: it looked as if Lance was about to finish what his ancestor would have liked to do.

He had nothing to ward off the bullets. The silver tray lay on the shop floor, forgotten in his haste to leave. He gripped the antique sword.

"You! And those brats!"

"Leave them out of it, Lance—your quarrel's with me. And you'd better not've hurt them."

"Ha! I left them for Nigel and Eddie to dispose of. You're mine."

Morehouse slowly tightened his grip on the sword handle and centered his weight, ready to spring.

Cumpston gave a thin smile. "You didn't do a very good job protecting your young friends. They never called the police, and Tommy phoned to say he lured them into the car, where all three of them fit nicely into the boot."

Morehouse had nothing to go on but sheer rage and willpower. At a distance of only about ten feet, Lance couldn't miss, but the first shot probably wouldn't kill him instantly. Might as well do some damage on the way down, maybe even take Lance with him.

The sound of the gun was deafening, and the pain in his head was stunning. Blood filled his eyes, but he didn't need to see or hear to find Lance. Instinct guided him forward, and he knew he was about to make contact when a fire erupted in his shoulder.

Then the world fell on top of him, and there was nothing.

Chapter Forty-five

Jagged pieces of consciousness stabbed at the pleasant curtain of blackness. Morehouse was on the floor, but someone was cradling his head and shoulders, wiping the blood from his eyes. His temporary deafness was replaced by a painful roar in both ears, and over it he heard a familiar voice.

"This is getting a bit tiresome."

He opened his eyes to slits, and gave a moan of despair: Tommy. But...there were police everywhere, and people carrying Lance away on a stretcher. And Tommy seemed to be in charge of it.

"What do you mean?"

"We just went through a similar drama with your young friends at the Soane Museum, though I'm pleased to report no one was shot."

"That's a relief. Just me, eh?"

"Two places, mate. A nice, clean hole through your shoulder. Bullet went right in and out—we collected it already. The other's a crease to your skull. Lots of blood, not much damage though, I think."

Morehouse struggled against the wave of nausea stirred by hearing about his own injuries. His ears were still ringing, and he couldn't tell if the voices of the other police were near or far away.

He complained, "Have you any idea how difficult it is to find a copper when you need one?"

Tommy chuckled. "I shouldn't wonder—we had the whole neighborhood cordoned off. Put out word through the media for folks to stay inside or stay away."

"What about Cumpston?"

"Hmph. He did some damage to himself on that sword, but he'll live."

"You mean he just fell on it—all by himself?"

"More or less. We came dashing in just as he was stepping forward to shoot you in the face. We startled him and ruined his aim, which is how your shoulder got clipped. You fell to the floor, still holding up the sword. I must say, your form was rather impressive. A single thrust at Cumpston, and he lost his footing. Fell on top of you and skewered himself. Nearly squashed you in the process." He scanned Morehouse's blood stained body. "Hurt a lot?"

Morehouse nodded and was grateful when a medic appeared at his side with an IV and bag. Almost immediately, the pain decreased and he drifted off to sleep.

Chapter Forty-six

Morehouse's hospital room was a mirror image of the one Liv had just left. During her overnight observation, a nurse had awakened her every thirty minutes to ask how she felt, and now she was ready for a nice, long nap.

Mrs. Wescott had spent the night on a cot by Liv's side, and she'd withheld questions so far. Her dad had probably grilled Anthony and Cal by now. As a lawyer, he'd know just how to do it.

He'd brought the boys with him to the hospital, and was downstairs with Mrs. Wescott, completing paperwork for her release. It gave Liv, Anthony and Cal a chance to "drop in and thank the nice man" who'd come to their aid: Morehouse.

"It's good to see you three," said Morehouse, wincing as he sat up in his hospital bed. "I expect to be discharged later today, and our paths might not cross again. Tommy—Inspector Harper —called, and he's dropping by for a visit. Or a grilling, depending on your point of view. I'm happy to tell him everything I know about Lance and company, but it's going to get a bit sticky explaining our friendship and how we came to be where we were.

I don't suppose you've spilled it all, or you'd probably be in a mental ward right now."

Liv bit her lip and looked at Anthony and Cal.

"We told my dad as much as we could," Anthony said. "It's true that we met in St. Augustine, bumped into each other here at the airport, and barely said hi. It's also true that Cumpston saw it and overreacted, and that he's a nutcase."

Anthony squirmed. "I lied to Dad about a few things, but it's true that Cumpston was spying and jumped to crazy conclusions. He did chase us for no good reason and you did risk your life to save us."

He ran his hand through his hair. "We might be able to avoid too many probing questions by acting traumatized, and that won't be much of an act."

The hospital door swung open. "Ah, the gang's all here."

Tommy—Inspector Thomas Harper—lumbered in and eased his bulky frame into a chair evidently made with only light-weight visitors in mind.

Liv heard shallow breathing. Her own. She did her best to look calm, while Anthony plunged in. "Wow! Thanks for saving me, Inspector Harper—that was cool!"

Here come the questions, she thought grimly, but the detective surprised her. "I suppose you're wondering what's been going on—I'll fill you in."

He turned to Morehouse. "And you can answer some questions later, if you're feeling up to it." Morehouse nodded.

He pointed to his broken nose. "I had this souvenir from my boxing days in school, but a run-in with a suspect a couple of years ago completed my gangster look, so to speak. That gave the Chief Inspector a brilliant idea: plant me undercover to infiltrate Cumpston's fraud network, before I had reconstructive surgery. The Kensington and Chelsea Council's Claims Investigation Group requested help some time ago, and our sting has been a year-long affair."

He grinned. "It's turned out so well that now he wants me to order up a completely different nose, get the birthmark removed, and embed myself in a new undercover operation, but that's another story. Last night, our team conducted a raid of several rented flats and residential hotels in the northeast Kensington area belonging to Lance Cumpston. We arrested Pridgeon and McKnickel, along with several tenants, the ones that tried the same scheme on their own, collecting their housing benefit cheques and subletting to illegals."

Liv held up a newspaper. "Dad brought a copy of the *Times* this morning. It looks like more of your crew were busy in Portobello Road yesterday while Cumpston was chasing us."

She read aloud:

"Trading Standards officers, accompanied by police, conducted an inspection of Portobello Road merchants and seized the inventory of the antiques firm of Cumpston, Pridgeon and McKnickel. An associate, Robert Morehouse, is wanted for questioning.   Though not officially a 'person of interest', Council officers would like to speak to Morehouse as part of their 'complete cleansweep'."

Liv lowered the paper and looked at the inspector.

Harper winked. "I think they won't be able to find him."

Liv continued reading:

"Unofficial estimates of Cumpston's housing fraud scheme alone range from ten thousand to twenty thousand pounds per week."

Harper shook his head. "Twenty-five's more like it, judging from what I saw."

Morehouse whistled. "That's well over a million pounds a year."

"And that's not even figuring in a penny from their shop or import/export business." He gave Morehouse a penetrating look. "Is there anything I should know?"

Morehouse squirmed in his hospital bed. "I sold a few high-priced items with less than solid provenance."

Harper raised his eyebrows.

"What's provenance?" asked Cal.

Morehouse offered, "It's proof of the history of a piece —the sort of stuff that affects the price." He made a show of straightening his sheet, discouraging more questions.

"That may not be ethical," said Harper, "but it's not technically against the law to be a smooth talker. If you mean deals like the Havards' armchair, they let you charm them into that one. You never actually said it was eighteenth century, or that it had been owned by royalty."

Morehouse's face reddened. "How did you—?"

"Homes, places of business and cars had more bugs than one of Cumpston's cheap hotel rooms. We even could record their mobile conversations."

"How about mine?"

Harper grinned. "Sorry, chum, we were on a budget and you weren't high priority. No offense."

"Well, that chair was authentic. I just couldn't prove it had been in the duke's townhouse, a gift from George the Third. Or that it stood in the drawing room."

Liv, sitting across from him on the sofa, caught the subtle upward curving of the outside of Morehouse's mouth and what he added: "But it was," he murmured.

"Yeah," answered Harper, "and the part about the cut on the chair's leg, and how it needed to be reupholstered in seventeen-seventy after a dinner attended by a genteel pirate who got into a little 'discussion' with a party-crasher who tried to stab him. That was a brilliant bit of hooey."

Morehouse pursed his lips and looked at the ceiling.

"No, Mr. Morehouse." The inspector leaned his bulky torso forward in the chair, the smile replaced by a serious look. "When I speak of crimes, I'm talking about the housing scams, because that's defrauding the government. And we'll soon have enough evidence to indict him for murder. Witnesses are popping out of the woodwork by the hour. They all want Cumpston and his helpers put away for a very long time."

He leaned back, folded his beefy hands on his lap, and waited.

Morehouse met the inspector's gaze directly. "I may not be able to prove I never participated and didn't know of their other crimes. They seemed to think I knew something. It's why they were after me—after us." He looked at the children. "It all started when he caught Liv watching him on the flight over here. He was paranoid, probably because he knew he couldn't hide what he was doing forever."

"That's more or less what we guessed, and Carmine Pridgeon has already assured us you had no part in the things we were investigating—a pretty good testimonial, as criminals usually try to pin everything on others they possibly can. Seems he was almost fond of you—tried to talk his partners out of eliminating you."

The inspector's serious look turned grave. "The others weren't so charitable—saw you as a necessary casualty of war. McKnickel, sniveling and trying to get the best deal for himself, is furious at you, you might want to know. Says you meddled in their business and got Cumpston all fired up. Says you'd be a marked man if Cumpston had any friends left, which I assured him he doesn't. We do have the recording of your last conversation with Cumpston, and I'd say that officially clears you."

Morehouse looked Inspector Thomas Harper in the eye. "I had no part in their schemes."

He nodded. "Just wanted to hear it from you. And if you've made any antiques deals that are a bit over the legal edge, it's likely no charges will be made, in appreciation of your unintentional help in drawing out Cumpston. It would have taken us longer to gather evidence if you hadn't provoked him."

He pointed at Morehouse. "Of course, that won't protect you from civil suits by clients who suspect you've sold them something other than what they paid for. You might want to contact anyone in question, try to work things out."

"I'll get right on it," said Morehouse. He cut his eyes toward Harper and smiled. "Speaking of antiques, you may have to seize Lance's inventory as evidence, but you'll want to get rid of it eventually. I'm happy to help."

"We'll see," answered the inspector in a voice that made it clear no unethical favors would be granted on his watch.

"Just one more thing—something we overheard on the tapes but couldn't make sense of. About your taking Cumpston to Barbados—you spoke as if you'd done it, which you obviously didn't."

A long pause followed. Harper slapped both hands on his knees and pushed himself to a standing position. "I've decided to believe it involved a client and let it go."

Walking to the door, he looked at all of them and settled his gaze on Liv. "For now, I'm also choosing to believe what you say about only just meeting Mr. Morehouse on that airplane, though my cop's instinct tells me there's more to it than that. But we don't need your testimony to convict Cumpston or any of his crew, and I'd rather not put a minor in harm's way over it. So, I'm dropping it."

He opened the hospital room door and paused. "For now."

Chapter Forty-seven

A glorious Sunday in Greenwich was passing all too quickly. The Wescotts and Cal, accompanied by Frederica, had played tourist all day, arriving early and taking in as many of the sights as time and energy allowed.

They'd marveled at the displays in the Maritime Museum, sneaked onto a portrait set in the Queen's House to snap photos of each other, and hiked up the winding path through Greenwich Park to the Observatory.

The Prime Meridian was back in place, solidly wedged into the pavement, full of tourists straddling both hemispheres and taking pictures. The guided tour of Flamsteed House was poignant: Liv knew things she couldn't tell, and longed to know other things she couldn't ask.

Did Maskelyne ever regret losing Precious? Did Octavius Cumpston get back to England and make a nuisance of himself?

She really couldn't complain about not having her questions answered. The four of them had squeaked by without having to reveal much about their own experiences. The Havards and Wescotts had assumed their children were simply in the wrong place at the wrong time and, on the advice of a police department counselor, let discussion of the matter of gun-wielding criminals drop, ready to listen only if any of them felt the need to talk.

Life had settled into a pleasant routine: sightseeing, running and doing footwork with the soccer ball in the parks, practicing the piano at Frederica's house four days a week.

The two girls were even playing duets. Frederica wasn't pounding the keys so hard these days, and Mrs. Havard had taken to hugging Liv every time she arrived.

While borrowing Anthony's laptop to email her debate team answers, Liv had done some Internet research on cutting. She'd learned that cutting could be a response to pressure or any bad feelings.

Some of the symptoms had Frederica written all over them: a feeling of not fitting in, a desire to take unnecessary risks and a tendency to be obsessive.

She was relieved to read that cutters don't usually mean to hurt themselves, but really want to feel better. There was hope, with family support and the right help.

Get her talking. That would be the way to start. But how?

Her chance came late that afternoon, at the Greenwich Sunday outdoor flea market. Tables, clotheslines, racks and chairs were laden with every used object imaginable, and Mrs. Wescott went into power-shopping mode.

The girls moved with the family group, then drifted away by themselves to a rack of clothing. "These shirts are pretty cool," said Liv. "The pink one would look good on you."

"Do you think I'm ready for short sleeves?"

"The small cuts have healed up fine. The question is: Do you want to keep hiding?"

Frederica twisted a strand of hair and spoke in a small voice. "I heard it talked about at school. Just some of the popular girls I never get along with, ridiculing weirdos who would do such a thing."

It was time to be Frederica's friend. The kind who listened, and even asked questions, if that's what it took to get her to open up. Liv smiled. "So, knowing you, you just had to try it yourself."

Frederica's posture stiffened, then she relaxed and returned the smile. "It was just something to do—only once, I thought, but the next time I felt awful about something Mum said to me, I tried it again."

The smile was replaced by tears. "Then Dad made a sarcastic remark about me that he thought I didn't overhear, and I just couldn't bear it. I knew I really shouldn't cut myself again, but I did. It's something of a habit now."

"Hey, I don't see any fresh cuts on those arms."

"You're right," Frederica said, her eyes widening. "I haven't done it for days—haven't even wanted to!"

"Congratulations! And you've talked to me about it. Now it's time to tell your mom."

Frederica crossed her arms and hunched over, staring at the ground. "I couldn't possibly," she whispered.

"Then how about another adult?" Liv racked her brain. "I guess your teachers and school counselors are out for the summer, but do you have a family doctor you can talk to? Maybe a neighbor or a relative? "Or how about writing your mom a note? I'll even help you write—"

"I'll talk to her myself, if you'll come with me."

Frederica was letting down the barriers. It was time for Liv to do the same. She reached out and took Frederica's hands in hers.

"Let's do it."

Chapter Forty-eight

The Havard house was filled with music and laughter, but for Liv, Anthony, Cal and Frederica, the atmosphere was bittersweet. Tomorrow was packing day, and Liv would be leaving a piece of her heart here in London.

People from Mr. Havard's law office had gathered to say goodbye to Mr. Wescott, and the Havards had graciously extended an invitation to Morehouse, at Frederica's request. Inspector Harper had promised to drop by later in the evening, if he could.

Morehouse was at his most charming. Even with a shoulder in a sling and a bandage on his head, he lit up the reception room, working the crowd of lawyers and making his way toward the four young people in the dining room, having secured a handful of appointments for antiques sales.

Inspector Thomas Harper slipped in, unremarkable in his wrinkled slacks and sportcoat. He passed up the serving plates and a tray of cauliflower-with-caviar hors d'oeuvres, piling his napkin with tiny quiches of bacon, apple and cheddar cheese. He leaned quietly against a wall, watching and listening.

Liv didn't interrupt Morehouse, but suspended her attention and gave Harper a smile. He acknowledged it with a wink.

Morehouse was saying, "The shopkeeper from the Silver Vaults has been very helpful, more than willing to testify against my assailants. And he offered me a good deal on the sword, which I just couldn't resist. I could sell it for twice that, to the right collector. But I think I may hang on to it—" he lowered his voice, "—for old times' sake."

He reached into a jacket pocket, pulled out a pack of business cards, and handed one to each of them. "Here—I've had new ones made up, but they're only temporary. My days in the antiques business are numbered—I miss the sea."

He squinted at Cal. "I don't know exactly why you suggested it in the airport that day, but the notion of returning to Florida and getting out on the water has been growing on me. A deep-sea fishing charter business would be just the ticket."

A frantic flapping of wings prevented more discussion. A green blur was knocked out of the air by a red one, and Precious swooped in and glided to a graceful landing on Morehouse's shoulder.

"Black Rob! Black Rob!" she crowed, hopping up and down.

Morehouse pulled her close and hissed, "Will you please shut up, you wretched tuft of feathers?"

"Shut up! Shut up, Black Rob!" she screamed.

"Well, that's not quite it," he said, rolling his eyes.

"Weigh anchor and hoist the mizzen, you old seadog!"

McGinty, recovered from his fall, joined her on Morehouse's other shoulder. "Scurvy dog! Scallywag!"

Morehouse looked from one to the other. "That's enough from the pair of you. That sort of language isn't acceptable in a proper house, so mind your manners."

Precious responded immediately with a bowed head, and McGinty reluctantly followed her example.

Inspector Harper appeared at Morehouse's side. "You have an unusual skill set," he drawled. "Swordsmanship, an uncanny knowledge of antiques, a very odd ability to attract parrots. I don't quite know what to make of you."

Morehouse grinned. "I don't quite know what to make of myself sometimes."

"Dead men tell no tales!" cried Precious.

Frederica clamped her fingers around Precious's beak. "She's absolutely bonkers. I do apologize."

"I'm on my way out anyway," said Harper. "Take care of yourselves." He waved to Morehouse. "See you at the trial."

He left them and made his way to Frederica's parents to say goodbye.

Morehouse sighed. "Ah, yes, the trial. At least it's not my own."

McGinty hopped from Morehouse's shoulder to Liv's head and began to pluck at the roots of her hair. "Ahoy! Ahoy! Batten down the hatches!"

Liv gritted her teeth while Frederica disengaged his zygodactyl toes from her scalp. "I can see he's forgotten how I saved his tailfeathers."

She studied Morehouse. "What's with you and Precious? She seems to know you awfully well."

"I'd rather not say," he replied primly.

She changed the subject. "You were telling us about quitting the antiques business. Won't you miss it?"

Morehouse slipped a piece of smoked salmon to Baxter, who had followed the birds out of the kitchen and expressed his disapproval of their behavior by locking eyes on them and growling. "I suppose."

Baxter forgot about the parrots and begged for more salmon. Morehouse obliged. "It's been fascinating to work in the Portobello Road Market area, knowing what it used to be like in my day. It might interest you to know that the name derives from one of the many exploits of a friend of mine—well, not a friend, precisely. More like a competitor."

Cal broke in. "You mean someone on the side of the law."

"You could put it like that. Admiral Vernon—Old Grog, he was called—captured the city of Puerto Bello, in Panama. Seventeen thirty-nine it was, and I assisted him by being only nine years old at the time and not yet a pirate.

"A winding country lane led to a farm, named Portobello by a patriotic farmer. A hundred years later, it was a favorite spot for people to gather on Saturday nights and watch side shows, have their palms read and pick up a bargain at the market."

He sighed. "And now it is what it is today. Nothing stays the same. My city's gone—I barely recognize it. All the people I knew are gone."

He stroked Baxter and allowed him to lick his salmon-flavored fingertips. "Visiting seventeen seventy-two made me realize that I don't belong there anymore either. But the sea—that's a friend that never lets me down. So I'll be on my way now. Stay in touch if you like."

He stood up straight and wiped his hands on his pants. "But don't go using that box again."

He offered his knuckles for fist bumps all around, gave a two-finger salute and walked out of the room, out of their lives again.

Chapter Forty-nine

The party was winding down. The music had stopped, and tables once piled high with food and drink were now filled with soiled dishes and glassware. Conversations continued, but they were subdued.

"Mom and Dad'll want to head out pretty soon," Anthony said to Frederica. "If you want to see your presents, you'd better come now. They're in the kitchen."

"Go on," said Liv. "We'll catch up in a minute."

She watched them disappear through the swinging door, then asked Frederica, "How's it going with your parents?"

"Better than I expected. We've started some counseling, and I think it's helping. I go by myself one day every week, and Mum and Dad go on another. If we do well, we'll get to try some sessions together."

"Oh, I think you will, and soon."

Frederica's smile lit up her face. "I believe you're right," she said. "Whatever our differences, they're my family—they stuck up for me in a crisis. Who knows? Maybe this year will be a good one at school, if I give people a chance, try to make some friends." She turned to hug Liv. "Thanks for helping me learn how to make a friend."

Liv returned the hug. "Same here."

In the kitchen, the four of them gathered, accompanied by the sounds of Precious and McGinty gnawing away at the fruit in the Wescotts' gift basket, a thank you to the Havards for letting Liv practice in their home.

Liv presented her gift first, and Frederica pulled off the ribbon and opened the box. "A short-sleeved blouse," she whispered, eyes shining.

Anthony nudged Cal, and the two of them pulled their baseball gloves from behind their backs. Anthony opened his to reveal a ball.

Frederica scratched at her cheek. "You're giving me your gloves?"

"It's an even better gift," Cal said proudly. "We're going to teach you how to catch a baseball! Meet us tomorrow morning in the park."

Frederica shook her head and laughed. "I'll be there. Wait—I have something for you, too."

She disappeared down the hallway and returned a minute later with a small box. "Here," she said, handing it to Liv. "I guess you'll have to work out how to share it. I could afford only just the one."

Liv lifted the lid of the cardboard box.

"Whoa!" breathed Anthony. "I know what that is—an H4 replica! Very cool!"

"It's perfect," said Liv. Cal nodded in agreement.

"And I bought it at the perfect place," she said. 'The First Shop in the World' now back in its proper place, at zero degrees longitude."

Chapter Fifty

The beginning of the return flight home was the only time a window seat would matter to Liv, so she'd bargained with the boys. It was hers for the first hour, then Anthony and Cal could split the rest of the time.

She planned to savor her last views of England. As the plane climbed into the sky, she wistfully watched the ground slip away. They skimmed over houses and highways, then soared higher and higher as the view changed to an achingly beautiful patchwork of emerald green fields dotted with sheep and bordered by stone fences.

She admired the scenery and considered how her life had changed in two short months. There'd been plenty of adventure, some incredible luck and too many close calls.

Carelessness with the Quimbaya secret and the box had almost cost the lives of two men, and the effects of going back in time to fix that had rippled into the present and almost gotten Morehouse and Anthony killed.

On the positive side, her most perplexing enemy, Frederica, was now a good friend. Both the Cumpstons were enemies, but she wasn't going to count them. Everyone was better off with Lance and his crew arrested, and though old Octavius hadn't appreciated it, she had helped keep him from becoming a murderer.

The only one she couldn't quite call a friend was McGinty, and after all she'd done for him! He'd continued to pester her up to the last minute, and Precious wasn't much better, squawking and urging him on with cries of, "Run a shot across the bow!"

At least they were happy with each other, and that made Liv smile. Maybe her happiness didn't depend on having everything fit her vision of perfection.

She'd practiced the piano well enough, stayed active and in shape, and kept up with her debate team. The positions she'd walked away from in June might be waiting for her when she got back.

If not, it was going to be okay. She wanted to be on the debate team—she no longer needed to be on it. And if someone else was soccer team captain—well, that might be a little harder to let go, but she could do it. And she had a friend she could talk to about it.

Her parents had invited Frederica to visit them in America next summer, and they had each other's email addresses.

She sat back in the seat as the plane continued its ascent, the beautiful English landscape now replaced by clouds. Then they left the clouds behind and sailed into the azure blue sky toward home.

About the Author

Dianne C. Stewart lives in Knoxville, Tennessee, with her husband, Tim, and teaches fourth graders. The characters in her stories are drawn from real life and her imagination. She wants her readers to believe in themselves and their ability to shape the future of the world. She invites them to visit her website at www.diannecstewart.com or to email comments and questions to her at dstewart8@bellsouth.net, with a book-related subject line.